By the same author

Louie's SOS

E. W. Hildick

Louie's SOS

Illustrated by Iris Schweitzer

Doubleday & Company, Inc., Garden City, New York

To John

who also answered
Louie's SOS

CONTENTS

Louie's SOS

Chapter 1

THE COMPLAINT

It had to come.

You can't be as good at your job as Louie without showing other people up. You can't show other people up without making enemies. And you can't make enemies without one of them, one day, trying to fix you, frame you, nobble you.

So it had to come. For Louie—Lewis Lay—was not only the best milkman in town. He was the best milkman in the British Isles. At delivering milk he was:

the quickest;

the most reliable (four feet of snow, floods, fog —these things might slow him up a bit, but he'd always get through with the milk);

the keenest;

the cleanest;

the most polite (always took his cigarette out
  when speaking to ladies over forty);

the cleverest; and

the most handsome.

Well, perhaps not *quite* the most handsome. He
didn't smile often enough to be that. In fact, he
didn't smile much at all. In fact—come to think of
it—nobody can remember him *ever* smiling. Just a
twitch of the lips now and then. And a special twirl
of the cigarette that was nearly always between
them. It was the cigarette that smiled, not Louie.

But he was tall and dark. He'd still quite a lot of black hair even though he was getting on for forty-five at the time all this happened. And thin. And he had this clean-shaved shiny look about his face—this polished look around the cheekbones—all hours of the day. And the same shiny look about his eyes too. Some of his enemies used to call it a *beady* look. Some of his friends used to agree. On the quiet. For there *was* something beady about Louie's eyes. Specially if he thought you'd messed up one of his deliveries. But that's life. You can't have everything. He wasn't *revolting* in looks—we'll put it that way.

There we have him, then: Louie Lay of the New Day Dairies, the best milkman in the country. And being best milkman doesn't just mean being best at delivering milk. Think. There's orange juice as well, for a start. And cream goes without saying. And the odd groceries that New Day go in for from time to time. And nylon stockings every so often. All the extra things that dairies do deal in these days.

Then there were all the private side lines that most milkmen have at one time or another. Where Louie scored was in having more than most. All at the same time. These included:

gathering and delivering mushrooms (in season);
collecting and delivering shoe repairs;
watch repairs the same;
and umbrella repairs;
also radio repairs;

repairs to broken dolls as well;

including false-teeth repairs (same-day service);

the delivery of sherry and other wines and spirits
   for shy old ladies (strict secrecy observed);

the delivery of racing tips in plain envelopes;

potatoes and other vegetables as available;

flowers, fresh-cut, to order;

and a special waking-up service, on request—
   using a knock that was not at all loud but
   guaranteed effective. Known only to Louie.
   Something to do with the rhythm.

Naturally Louie was only the go-between in most
of these things. *He* didn't do any of the repair work
himself. *He* didn't grow the flowers or vegetables.
He didn't bottle the sherry or tip the winners. But
he knew people who did these things—people who
could be relied upon—and he knew customers who
wanted them. And so long as they got their milk
from New Day Dairies, Louie was happy to oblige.
He used to tell his boys: "I'd do it for nothing—
just to oblige a customer."

But, of course, nobody ever asked him to do these
things for nothing.

Which brings us to Louie's greatest triumph.
Those boys. The boys he had working on the route
with him. Hand-picked. Specially trained. Louie's
Lot.

This was what people used to call them. "Louie's
Lot," they used to say. "Oh, he's one of Louie's Lot."

Or: "He used to be one of Louie's Lot. You can tell by the way he works."

At any one time there would only be two boys on the actual route with him—which doesn't sound a *lot*. But there were always four or five lads on the evening paper route that Louie used to run—lads who had started on the milk route. And then there were two with Sid, the other milkman, himself an ex-member of Louie's Lot. All of them had been picked and trained by Louie—and it was this training that did it. This was Louie's greatest triumph. To be trained by Louie was like a cross between going on a commando course and spending a year at Jesus College, Cambridge. It did something to a boy—physically and mentally.

"Yer!" they'd probably say, if you asked them. "It gives you blisters on your fingers and makes you dream of bottles."

But that's only if you asked the boys actually on the route *now*—Tim Shaw and his friend Smitty. You ask any of the older ones, the members of Louie's Lot who've grown up, and they'll tell you a different tale. But have a checkbook ready. It costs a dollar or two to speak to some of those boys now. They include:

a bank manager;
a lawyer;
a City Mayor (straight—no fooling);
two newspaper reporters;

an international soccer player (dropped after his
  second game, but he should never have been
  put on the wing);
a detective sergeant;
an Army officer;
a chemist;
a veterinarian;
an electronics engineer;
three teachers;
a famous actor;
a parson; and
a writer of books (not famous yet, but coming on
  fast).

In fact, Louie was talking about one of these old
boys when the ax fell that morning. There he was,
cigarette in mouth, sleeves rolled up, the tattooed
birds on his left arm seeming to flit in and out of the
tattooed letters, N.D.D., on his right arm, as he
helped Tim and Smitty sort out the empties at the
corner of Booth Crescent and Booth Drive, just after
7:45. Like the flailing arms of a windmill, Louie's
arms went up, across, over, crash, as he restacked
the crates of empties on the back of the truck.

"C'm on! 'S matter with yer? Slow 's morning,
en't yer?" he was saying to Tim and Smitty as they
sweated to keep up. "Not like Norbert Rigg. Best
stacker I ever had."

"Norbert Rigg?" said Tim. There was wonder in
his voice. This was the famous actor. Seven big

movies and four wives already, and only twenty-six years old.

Now Tim was being crafty here. *He* knew Norbert Rigg had once been one of Louie's Lot, all right. Who didn't? But Tim was fairly new to the route. He thought that if he could get Louie talking, the man would slacken off. Tim thought Louie was like some of the teachers at school—get 'em chatting, then sit back and rest.

Smitty knew different. He rolled his eyes and gave a little groan and jabbed Tim with his elbow. But it was too late.

"Yer! Norbert Rigg!" grunted Louie, going faster than ever—crash, over, up, across, crash . . . It was as if the mention of his prize pupil had inspired him. "Old Nobby Rigg. Every time I see him"—crash! across, bash!—"I remember him stacking his crates . . ." Crash! bash! "That last picture of his, with that blond bird, rescuin' her from them East German guards . . ." With sweat rolling into their ears as they tried to keep up, the boys could hardly make out what he was saying . . . *"That* reminded me of when he used to stack these crates . . ." *Crash!* "That bit where he chucked her over the barbed-wire fence." *Crash!* "That was the one where he played eight different parts. Allus was good at taking people off." *Crash!* "Come *on!* What yer waiting for?"

Yes. Beady Louie's eyes were, sure enough, as

they glared at Tim and Smitty then, through the rising smoke of his cigarette.

"We—huh—we——"

But Smitty's excuse, whatever it was—and it was probably a good one—never got uttered. For just then, with a squeal of brakes, up came one of the dairy's cars with Mr. Peters, deputy manager, at the wheel.

"Hello?" murmured Louie. "'S *he* want?"

His eyes weren't beady any more. They'd narrowed to needle points. It was just as if Louie could sense that something really awful had happened.

"Louie!" gasped Mr. Peters, a little plump man. "For heaven's sake . . . Louie!"

It was as if he'd been running, he was so out of breath.

"Yer?" said Louie, giving the bluebirds on his left arm a nervous scratch. "Dairy on fire or something?"

"Worse!" groaned Mr. Peters, looking as if he was going to be sick out of the window. "Much worse! We've—we've just had a complaint—phone—Mrs. Bellamy—Albion Grove—she's—she's——"

"Yer?"

Louie's cigarette had burned right down to his lips. It seemed as if at any moment the bright burning blob would be sucked in. But Louie didn't seem to notice. He was too busy staring at Mr. Peters. If there was anything Louie hated it was a complaint. To have forgotten to leave an extra pint was terrible. To have left the wrong kind, disaster.

Mr. Peters daren't look at him. He looked wildly

at Tim and Smitty instead. His eyes rolled, as if appealing for help.

Then all at once he closed them. The world, just then, was too much for him to face.

"She's found something in the milk," he moaned.

There was a hiss. The boys looked up at Louie. He was groping under his sweater for another cigarette. There was no sign of the last one now. Probably he's sucked it in, thought Tim. Burning end and all.

"Go on," said Louie, in a strange choking voice. "What? What's she found? Bit of a torn-off bottle cap or something?"

It was wishful thinking. Must have been. Louie must have sensed that it was something worse than that.

But he couldn't have known just how worse.

Mr. Peters shook his head, like a drowning man coming up for the third and last time. Still with his eyes shut, he said:

"No, I wish it *had* been. I only wish it had . . . But . . . but . . . Louie, she says when she opened it, careful not to spill any cream—these are her own words—she saw what looked like a *lump* of cream. Clotted. So . . . so she took a spoon, thinking to scoop it out and save it for the fruit for tea . . . And . . . Louie . . . it *wasn't* a lump of clotted cream. It was too big. Too long. Too—too rubbery . . . It was —she found it out when she started scraping it—it was a *goldfish* . . . Dead."

21

Chapter 2

THE DEAD GOLDFISH

What did Louie do then? How did he take the dreadful news? How did he take the full force of Mr. Peters' news?

At the word "goldfish" he blinked.

At the word "dead" he blinked again.

After blinking the second time he kept his eyes shut—which made it only half a blink really.

Then he took a deep slow breath.

It was so deep that it made his fresh cigarette glow like the end of a fuse. It made it glow and creep. The glowing end crept steadily nearer and nearer to his mouth. The more it crept the brighter it glowed. This must have been because he was taking the deep slow breath up his nose as well. His nostrils must have been sucking up all the ash as soon as it was made. His nostrils must have been acting as a vacuum cleaner—keeping the glowing creeping end of his cigarette nice and bright.

Everything about him seemed to be creeping, moving, going through a change. He didn't wave his arms about. He didn't clutch his hair. He didn't stamp. He didn't shout. He just breathed in deeply on the spot. He just stood where he was, seeming to grow.

He seemed to grow thinner. He seemed to grow taller. His hair seemed to grow blacker. His nose seemed to grow more hooked. His face went shinier, the skin of it seeming to grow tighter. It was as if some parts of his growing went faster than others. That must have been why he went shinier—the cheekbones growing faster than the skin.

And the things *on* him seemed to be affected too. As Louie breathed in deep and slow, and started growing on the spot, the bluebirds on his arm and the stags on his sweater seemed to be stirred too.

We have mentioned the tattooed bluebirds. As Louie breathed in deep and his cigarette glowed brighter, the bluebirds seemed to soar like hawks. Then swoop. Then soar again.

But we haven't mentioned the stags before. They were there in the pattern on his blue and white sweater. As Louie breathed in deep and slow and grew on the spot, eyes closed, cigarette glowing, the stags began to fight. They drew back, charged,

24

locked antlers. Drew back, charged, locked antlers . . .

That was how Louie took the first full force of
Mr. Peters' awful news.

He mustered his strength.

He mastered his feelings.

Only the cigarette and the stags seemed to suffer.

It couldn't last, of course, and it didn't last. But
while Louie stood mustering and mastering, what
about the others?

What did Tim and Smitty do?

Kept quiet, for a start.

Dreadful though the news was, it was not as
dreadful as the sight of Louie just then. So they kept
quiet and thanked heaven the complaint had come
from Louie's own particular part of the route. He
used to start at 4:30 A.M. They didn't join him till
6:30 A.M. This was the law. And they had never felt
so thankful for that law as they did then. Because
Albion Grove came in the earlier part of the route,
they couldn't be blamed in any way.

But they kept quiet, all the same.

And what did Mr. Peters do?

He kept quiet at first as well. He might have been
deputy manager, but this didn't really put him above
Louie. Louie could have been deputy manager ten
times over. He could have been manager nearly as
many times over. But he was too good a milkman
to waste his time in an office. He was much too
valuable to New Day Dairies to promote to an office

job. So they kept him on the route and paid him more than a manager, and everybody was pleased. Some say that they had even made him a vice-president on the quiet, years before.

So Mr. Peters minded what he said and did. And what he said at last, very softly, was, "Well, we thought we'd better leave it to you to sort out, Louie." And what he did was drive off fast as soon as he'd said it.

So what did Louie do *next?*

It's easy to ask. Like most questions it is easier to ask than answer. But think for a minute. What would *you* have done next?

It was a tricky thing to decide. It was like one of those puzzles you see in kids' books. Particularly it was like that Dog and Geese and Farmer one. The one with the boat. This farmer wanting to cross the river and there's only enough room in the boat for himself and one of the two geese. And this dog of his, licking its lips at the thought of being left alone for a while with a goose or two. And the old farmer having to decide how to get 'em all across without giving the dog the chance it wants. And how does he do it? How many journeys? Which went with him first? All that. . . .

Louie's problem wasn't quite so bad. Neither Tim nor Smitty was likely to get busy and drink the milk while he was away. Louie wasn't worried about that. What he was worried about was how to deal with the complaint before the woman could make it to the Health Inspector, yet waste as little time as possible with the rest of the deliveries. So did he:

1. Take the truck and both boys direct to Albion Grove?

2. Send one of the boys to deal with the complaint and get on with the deliveries himself?

3. Leave both boys with the truck and the milk and go on foot to Albion Grove while they got on with the delivering?

4. Take the truck and one of the boys with him as a witness?

5. Take the truck and one of the boys, after unloading enough crates for the remaining boy to deliver at the next three streets?

The answers are: 1. What, and hold up all the deliveries? 2. Don't be stupid. Talking a way out of this one was going to call for all Louie's cunning. 3. Too far away. 4. Warmer. 5. But of *course*. . . .

It took about an hour to write that problem down. It probably took about two minutes to read it. But it took Louie only about five seconds to go through the lot and decide. Five seconds after he'd stopped mustering his strength and breathing in and burning up his cigarette.

"C'm on," he said—crash! (that was the first crate landing on the pavement). "Don't just stand there gapin'." Crash! (That was the second.) "Help us off with a dozen er these." Crash! crash! "You carry on here, Smitty." Crash! "This radio's for num-

ber 29." Cr—— just in time Louie remembered that
the newly mended radio wasn't a crate of bottles.
He laid it gently on top of the unloaded pile. Then
he spat out what was left of his cigarette, said, "C'm
on, you! Get in!" to Tim, jumped in the cab, and
drove off.

Time: 25 seconds flat.

He spoke only twice all the way to Albion Grove.
The first thing he said was: "Whatever happens
we got to settle it now. Before she calls the City
Hall."

The second thing he said was: "An' you keep yer

trap shut. I'll do the talking. You just listen and keep yer eyes open."

What Tim was supposed to keep his eyes open *for*, Louie didn't say. And there wasn't time to ask, because when he said it they'd just pulled up outside Mrs. Bellamy's house.

The woman was at the window, looking very pale.

When she saw the truck her lips went tight.

And when she came to the door the saucer was in her hand, with the fish laid across it, glinting golden in a pool of cream.

Chapter 3

LOUIE ASKS QUESTIONS

"A fine thing!" said Mrs. Bellamy.

She was staring up at Louie. Louie and Tim were staring down at the fish. The fish stared back at Louie with its one cold eye.

Mrs. Bellamy wasn't praising the fish, of course. She might have caught it, but she wasn't proud of it. And it wasn't the fish itself that she thought was fine. It was finding it in her milk. And what she really meant was the opposite of fine.

That's where a foreigner might have come unstuck. Anyone not familiar with the English language might have made a big mistake. He might have agreed with her. He might have praised the fish for its beautiful color. He might have said: "Yes, madam—and what a lovely tail it's got."

And that would have been that.

For Mrs. Bellamy was a woman in two minds. She liked her food clean. And she loved animals. She hadn't been sure whether to send for the Health Inspector or the SPCA. Still undecided, she had split the difference and called the dairy.

But one false move, one wrong word, one flicker of amusement or disbelief and she'd have called the first. She'd have sent for the Health Inspector and left him to sort it out.

So Louie was very respectful. He'd pinched out his cigarette at the garden gate and put it in his pocket. He didn't even risk sticking it behind his ear.

"This is terrible, Mrs. Bellamy," he said. "Terrible."

And, of course, he meant it. The word came out like the mutter of distant thunder.

There's nothing like sincerity. Mrs. Bellamy's eyes flickered behind her glasses. Her expression softened a bit.

"Come in while I tell you," she said.

Then she went through it all again, everything that Mr. Peters had said she'd said before. With trimmings about what sort of fruit she'd been thinking of having the cream with (raspberries) and so on.

Louie let her go on. He listened to everything she said. You'd have thought it was someone telling him the secret of winning a million, the way Louie listened. And when Tim once looked like chipping in he got such a look from Louie's left eye (he kept the right eye on the lady) that the boy nearly passed out.

When she had finished, Louie asked his questions. Leaving out all the times he politely murmured "madam" and "Mrs. Bellamy" and putting in only a sprinkling of them, the interview went on like this:

"Did you notice anything wrong, madam? With the bottle? When you took it in?"

"Well, no. Not that I can think of."

"The cap, Mrs. Bellamy—was it loose at all?"

"Well, I don't really know. I wouldn't like—"

"Have you still got it?" (This was Tim's question.)

"Shaddap when the lady's speakin'!" (That was Louie's reply to it.) "I'm sorry, Mrs. Bellamy. I'll have to learn him his manners later . . . You was sayin' about the cap . . . ?"

But Mrs. Bellamy couldn't be sure.

"I see," said Louie. "Well, perhaps you kept it, did you?" (With a look at Tim as if to say, "There's a right an' wrong time for every question"—and another look to add: "An' a right and wrong way of asking it!")

Mrs. Bellamy went into the kitchen. She went to the sink. Louie and Tim followed.

"Yes!" cried Mrs. Bellamy. "Here!"

She fished it out of the sink strainer. She turned on a faucet, ready to wash it.

"No!!" yelped Louie. "Madam!" he added quickly. "Fingerprints," he explained, holding out his hand-kerchief. "Just drop it on there an' we'll have it examined."

"Good heavens!" gasped the lady. She dropped it as if it had been red-hot. Louie caught it on the handkerchief and gently wrapped it up. "You don't think someone's been messing about with the bottle, do you?" she asked. "*Here?* While it was on the doorstep?"

"I don't think, lady—I *know*," said Louie grimly. "While we was at the door I looked on the step. First thing I see. A ring of cream an' a bit of a pool." He turned to Tim. "You see it?"

Tim shook his head.

"Ner!" grunted Louie, giving him another look. "Like I said: the closer you keep yer trap, the wider you can get yer eyes." He turned to Mrs. Bellamy and his voice changed. "But just come and see for yourself, madam . . ."

They went to the door. There was the ring of cream, just the size of the bottom of a bottle. A cat's tail just disappearing around the corner told where the extra small pool had gone.

"But couldn't it have been *you?*" asked Mrs. Bellamy. "Just spilling it a bit when you put it down?"

Anyone else asking that question—any man or boy —would have done well to put it in writing. Then he'd have done even better to post it and be sure to leave the district. Tim cringed for Mrs. Bellamy then. But Louie was a model of politeness. All he said was:

"Madam, that is something I have never done yet."

Mrs. Bellamy took it. But she still looked worried.

"But who would do a thing like that?" she said. "Sneak up here and do a thing like that?"

"I don't know exactly," muttered Louie. "Only I've one or two ideas."

"But we've no children, we're friends with all the neighbors, we——"

This time Louie did interrupt. In this case, though, it was a perfectly polite interruption. He did it to spare her feelings.

"It's not *you* they'd be getting at, Mrs. Bellamy," he said. "It's *us—me* . . ."

For a second it looked as if his politeness would break down. But he was a man of iron, Louie. Polished steel.

"Don't stand there," he said to Tim. "Go an' fetch Mrs. Bellamy a fresh pint to take this one's place. An' a bottle of that special heavy cream . . . And is there a can of mixed fruit left?"

He gave a little bow as Tim handed over the two bottles and the can.

"The cream and fruit with the dairy's compliments, madam," he purred. "And now, if you don't mind, we'll take the—er—first bottle—and the fish—and we'll get the matter looked into."

35

Then, carrying the tampered-with bottle with the sleeve of his sweater pulled over his hand, they went back to the truck. Tim felt a bit of a fool with the fish itself in *his* handkerchief. "All we need are some french fries!" he felt like saying.

But the look on Louie's face told him he'd better not bother.

Chapter 4

MORE TROUBLE

That was the start of the worst week in New Day Dairy's history. That was the start of the worst week in Louie's history. That was the start of a week Louie could never look back on without breaking into a sweat.

For that was only the first of a whole string of complaints.

The very next morning brought another three. Three more complaints about things found in bottles of milk or cream. These were: two cigarette butts (each in a different bottle at a different house) and a shoestring (brown, with a knot in it).

The day after that brought three more. These were: the hour hand of a small clock (or it might have been the minute hand of a large watch); a raincoat button; and a milk note on a strip torn off a cigarette packet. The milk note read: *Two extra pints after today please.* Underneath it the angry customer had written: *No more milk from YOU after this—ever. Thank you.*

On the next day the crop was the biggest of the lot. In different bottles at different houses there were found:

one finger bandage;
half a cuff link (stainless steel with a diamond pattern);
one piece of broken glass;
one wad of pink chewing gum (chewed); and
one beer-bottle cap.

Not all the complaints came through while Louie was on the route. Some did. In fact Tim and Smitty got to be quite nervous, listening out for Mr. Peters' car. But some came later in the day, as the customers got around to opening fresh bottles. And one came through at eleven o'clock at night. That was the raincoat button—after the customer's wife had nearly knocked a hole in his back getting him to cough it up.

But *when* the complaints came in is not important. What *is* important is the fact that Louie wasn't always successful at calming the people. He wasn't always as successful as he had been with Mrs. Bellamy.

The milk-note people, for example. They were a write-off as soon as they'd made the complaint. They sent the scrap of damp cardboard around to the dairy, of course. But with the angry message already quoted.

The raincoat-button man was in no mood to be pacified, either. He was going to hang on to that button and wait to see if he'd been poisoned. If he had, then the dairy could look out. In the meantime he was going to get his milk elsewhere.

The finger bandage was anybody's guess. That customer was out when Louie called. A neighbor said she'd had hysterics when she found it. She'd gone off to her sister's for a day or two to get over it. Somewhere in the country. Where the milk came straight from the cows.

One of the cigarette butts and the shoestring were sports. They handed the articles in and said anybody could make mistakes. But they hoped it wouldn't happen again.

The half cuff-link customer was crafty. For a week's free delivery she'd return the article to the dairy and nothing more would be said. The broken piece of glass customer was even craftier. If Louie would scrub the two weeks' money she owed and let her off the next two, that would be all right.

As for the rest it was wait and see. Like the raincoat-button man, they canceled their orders. Like him, they hung on to the articles. Like him, they said they'd wait to see if they had any ill effects. If they did it would be heaven help the dairy. These were the customers who'd found:

the other cigarette butt;
the minute hand of the watch (she was chiefly worried about what had happened to the other hand);
the wad of chewing gum; and
the beer-bottle cap.

That was bad enough. It was like having a lot of loaded guns trained on you—as Louie, Smitty, and Tim soon realized. But to make matters worse, these big complaints gave rise to a lot of small ones.

There was the general nervousness for a start. The boys found they couldn't bring themselves to put a bottle on a doorstep without looking at it closely. Without turning it slowly around and around. Without tilting it carefully this way and that. Without testing the cap with their fingernails to make sure it was on firmly. True, so far all the complaints were coming from Louie's solo part of the route. But Tim and Smitty were uneasy. And all the testing and tilting and turning made them slower. So complaints began to come in about late deliveries.

Louie himself couldn't grumble about this. For one thing he was just as uneasy as the boys. There were some bottles he spent up to a minute on— each—before finally putting them down. And for another thing he was getting to be late in any case.

Two mornings running he'd been ten minutes late

picking up the boys. This was because on his own part of the route he'd spent so much time doubling back. He still suspected that the bottles were being tampered with. So, in the hope of catching the culprit, he kept doubling back to where he'd already delivered. Peeping around corners. Hiding behind bushes. Cursing quietly and going through his cigarettes twice as fast.

Especially did he suspect the rival firm—Rely-On-Us Dairies. Whenever their truck was around he spent more time watching their boys than he did watching Tim and Smitty. But he couldn't catch them doing anything wrong. He couldn't even claim that it proved anything when the Rely-On-Us milkman, Bertie Winks, sniggered and said: "Hear yer having a lot of complaints lately, Louie!" After all, the news was bound to get around. And some customers were beginning to change to Rely-On-Us even before they'd got hurt.

So that was how it was at the start and in the middle of that black week for Louie and the dairy. Then, toward the end, the complaints tailed off. The big complaints, that is. The small ones, for lateness, grew, if anything. (This was because of the uneasiness and Louie's doubling back. He kept switching suddenly off his usual course, even when the boys were with him. He kept making sudden drives back into the early part of the route.)

But the big complaints—yes, they dwindled. Friday there was none at all. And on the Saturday morning, as they arrived back at the dairy at the end of the route, Louie was beginning to look his old self again. Not so haunted. Not so anxious. Not so uneasy. Merely moody.

"It looks like we're getting out of this patch," he said, driving into the yard. "It looks like we can start catching up again," he said, stopping the truck. "It looks——"

He paused with his hand on the door.

"—like——" he went on, slow now, dead slow, peering through his cigarette smoke at the general office window and a man inside, standing with his back to it.

"—that Health Inspector!" he groaned, flinging his cigarette down and stamping on it. "What's *he* want?"

Chapter 5

THE SUMMONS

"You'll see some sparks fly now, mate!" said Smitty in a whisper. He was plucking Tim's sleeve. "Just stand back and give 'em room, mate!" he said, as Louie marched toward the office. "Talk about fireworks! *Mamma mia!*"

Tim was newer to the job than Smitty. He had enough to do studying Louie's moods and methods without going into his life story. He had enough on his plate studying Louie's likes and dislikes *now*, in the present. As far as Tim was concerned the past could take care of itself.

But if he'd listened to Louie carefully a few seconds ago, he might have guessed there was something special blowing up.

For Louie hadn't said: "It looks like *the* Health Inspector." He hadn't said: "It looks like *a* Health Inspector." He had said: "It looks like *that* Health Inspector."

That.

With feeling.

As Tim found out later, there'd been trouble before between that particular inspector and Louie. Nobody was sure exactly what it was about. Some said it had something to do with Louie smoking on the route. Others said no—it had all started over Louie's side lines. They said the inspector had objected to Louie's repairs being taken around on the same truck as the milk. They said he objected to secondhand objects getting taken around with the milk. Dusty old radio sets. Dusty old teddy bears, full of germs.

Anyway, whatever it was, neither of the men had actually *won.* Louie still kept on smoking. He still kept on with the repairs. But he used to take good care to put out his cigarette if ever he caught sight of that particular Health Inspector (whose name was Dabbit). And he always used to take good care to carry the repairs in a separate box in the cab.

Some said it would have been better if one or the other *had* actually won. The thing would have been settled then. The one who'd won would have been satisfied. The one who'd lost could have pretended there'd never been any argument, anyway. As it was —well—they hated each other's guts. And not only

did they hate each other's guts. They hated each
other's:

livers;
kidneys;
hearts;
lungs;
gullets, windpipes, nostrils;
ear tubes;
tonsils;
teeth, tongues; and (moving outwards)
lips;
chins;
all warts, moles, and other birthmarks;
arms, hands, fingers, thumbs;
legs, knees, kneecaps, shins, ankles; and
feet.

They didn't stop at basic personal things, either.
They hated the clothes each other wore. Dabbit
hated Louie's sweater even unto the tips of the stags'
antlers. Louie hated Dabbit's greeny-browny suits.
Dabbit loathed Louie's long black shoes. Louie de-
tested Dabbit's stubby little brown ones. (And in
hot weather Dabbit's sandals used to make Louie
chatter softly with fury.)

Dabbit was wearing sandals now.

The two men met at the door, just as the Health
Inspector was leaving.

Mr. Peters was at his side and a little behind,
looking very pale.

Tim and Smitty were at Louie's side and a little behind, looking very interested.

It was a strange scene.

Louie was tall, dark, thin.

Dabbit was short, brown, rather plump.

Louie's face was long and moody.

Dabbit's face was round and peevish.

Louie's face had this shine about it—now a menacing shine.

Dabbit's face had a chalky look, clean but powdery, chubby but not smooth. Think of the skin on top of one of those soft cheeses when it's getting rather stale, give it a nasty sort of sneer, and you'll have the face of Gilbert Dabbit.

And they hated each other so much they couldn't bear to look at each other for long.

"Ah! Here's the man whose route it was on," said Dabbit, looking straight at Smitty.

"Whose route *what* was on?" said Louie, looking straight at Mr. Peters.

"The subject of the summons," said Dabbit with a little smirk, still looking at Smitty.

"The—*summons?*" said Louie, glaring at Mr. Peters. He took out a cigarette and lit it fast. He couldn't help it.

"Yes, under the Clean Food Act," said Dabbit, this time frowning at Smitty.

"What the—what for, then?" said Louie, looking daggers at poor Mr. Peters—who closed his eyes and shuddered.

"A bottle of milk," said Dabbit slowly, fixing Smitty with an accusing stare that made the boy squirm. "A pint bottle of milk," went on Dabbit, a note of triumph creeping into his voice—and that made *Louie* squirm. "A pint bottle of milk that has been found to contain three teeth."

Smitty gave a little yelp. Louie ground his own teeth. Tim was a good two yards away, but he could hear them being ground.

"Yer what?" jeered Louie, looking Mr. Peters up and down with deep contempt. "Talk sense, man."

But his ears had gone red.

"Three teeth," said Dabbit, scowling at Smitty, as if they were all in court already and the boy had rudely interrupted the judge. "False teeth. A row of three. Part of an upper set of dentures."

"And the dairy's being summonsed," moaned Mr. Peters, speaking for the first time. He glanced at a folded sheet of blue paper in his hand. "On the tenth of next month," he added.

"At the hour of two in the afternoon," continued Dabbit, who knew it all by heart and recited it as if it were the sweetest poetry he'd ever heard. "Before the court of Summary Jurisdiction——"

"Mind yer language in front of these boys!" snapped Louie at Mr. Peters.

"—at the City Hall," said Dabbit, giving Smitty a look that dared him—just *dared* him to be late.

Then, with a smirk for Mr. Peters and Tim, he wished them a good day, stepped around the stricken Louie, and left them to it.

For fully two minutes Louie didn't move. He just stood there glaring at Mr. Peters, cigarette glowing furiously. For fully two minutes he stood there like some tall bare tree that has been struck by lightning. Still tall, still strong, but struck slightly crooked—with one charred twig still smoldering.

Then Mr. Peters coughed and turned and sighed. He pushed open the door.

"Come in and have a cup of tea," he said. "Let me tell you exactly what's happened."

It was only too clear what had happened, of course. There was hardly any need for Mr. Peters to explain.

48

What had happened was that Louie's luck hadn't held, after all. What had happened was that at last a customer had phoned straight through to the City Hall. What had happened was that Dabbit had been only too glad to rush straight over. What had happened was just what Louie had been afraid of.

Whoever had been tampering with the milk had succeeded. Louie had been fixed, framed, nobbled.

"Of course it's the *dairy* who's been prosecuted," said Mr. Peters, glancing again at the summons and chewing his bottom lip.

"Yer, I know," grunted Louie. "But it's me who'll have to go and answer for it."

And *his* lips were so tight he'd have broken his teeth trying to chew either of them.

He'd been nobbled, all right. Oh yes—Louie Lay had been nobbled this time and no mistake.

Chapter 6

RUMORS

That was the *end* of the blackest week in Louie's life.

The blackest up to then, that is.

For the following week was blacker still. In fact, it was so black that it made the first seem golden. It made it seem like a golden age. It made it seem as golden as the scales of the fish that had started it.

The first week had contained all the causes of trouble. The second week contained the effects. With causes of trouble you still have a chance. There's still a chance that nothing very bad will come of them. There's still a chance that by dashing around in circles you can put things right. There's still a chance that by working twice as hard and smoothing things over and handing out extra jars of heavy cream, you can get yourself into the clear again. You may not think much of these chances. You may have your doubts. But at least the chances are there.

With effects there's no such hope. Effects—in a case like this—are just what you'd been hoping wouldn't happen. The summons itself was one of them. It came at the end of the week of causes. It signaled the beginning of a week of other effects. And some of these were even worse. Like the rumors. Like the black ugly rumors that began to spread around the town at the beginning of the second week.

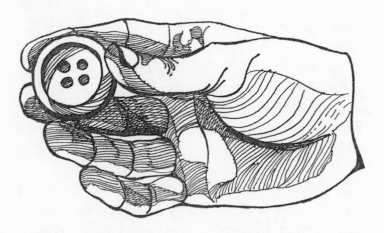

Now let's get this straight. Let's just go over the list of what actually *had* been found in Louie's bottles. There was the dead goldfish for a start.

Then (though not necessarily in this order) there came:

two cigarette butts;
the shoestring;
the clock (or watch) hand;
the milk note;
the finger bandage;
the raincoat button;
the half cuff link;
the wad of chewing gum;
the piece of broken glass;
the beer-bottle cap; and the
three false teeth.

That was the full score of objects actually found. And you might think that was bad enough.

But when rumor got to work, rumor added the following:

one policeman's whistle;
two baby shoes;
one lock of yellow hair, tied with pink ribbon;
three dead mice;
eight brass nails;
four flashlight batteries;
three old wrist-watch straps;
two broken ball-point pens; and
one live snake in a plastic bag.

It was just like that song about the days of Christmas and what my true love sent to me. Except there wasn't much love in it. And nothing true.

"I mean," said Louie bitterly, going over the list around Wednesday. "It stands to sense. How could a snake *live* in a plastic bag in a bottle of milk? An' who's gonner leave baby shoes in a bottle? Who's gonner *put* 'em in an empty bottle in the first place—just supposin' it is an accident?"

"*You* might," mumbled Smitty, dodging behind the crates they were stacking.

"Eh?" snapped Louie.

The bluebirds were soaring, ready to swoop with deadly accuracy in the direction of Smitty's right ear hole.

"I—I'm not saying you *would*," said Smitty, talking fast. "What I mean, I mean I been thinking. Some of these things—I mean some of these things that they really did find—well—they're connected, en't they?"

Louie's bluebirds still looked as if *they* might be about to connect. But then Louie grunted and smoothed his hair back instead.

"See what yer mean," he said. "*I* been wondering about that too."

"See what?" asked Tim. "Wondering about what?"

Danger over, Smitty was a bit cocky now.

"You're slow, mate, en't yer? Shoestrings and that. Batteries and that. Broken pens. Brass nails. Note that—*brass* 'uns. Watch straps. That clock hand. Baby shoes. False teeth. Yer—even that hair—folk might think it's *doll's* hair . . ."

"Oh, I see!" said Tim. "You mean connected with Louie's repairs? Things that seem *likely?*"

"Yer!" grunted Louie, putting down a crate with a quite unnecessary slam. "And another likely thing— when I catch the bloke who's at the back of all this —is his . . ."

But what part of the culprit's body or belongings Louie was thinking of, he didn't say. Maybe he wasn't sure himself. Maybe he was spoiled for choice.

All he did say was: "C'm on. Move it. Talkin's not gonner get the milk delivered."

This was more like the usual Louie, of course. This was the spirit that had made him the best milkman in the country. But even by then, even by the Wednesday of that week, it was beginning to look as if there soon wouldn't be much milk to *be* delivered. Not by him, anyway.

This was because the rumors and the real complaints were, between them, getting on with *their* work. Toward the end of the first week there had seemed to be a lull. Things had looked black, but not all that black. True, about a dozen customers had canceled their orders and switched to Rely-On-Us. But it had looked as if the worst was over.

Now, during the second week, the cancellations suddenly increased. Apart from the rumors, everyone in town seemed to know about the summons. Even though the case itself was still four weeks off, everyone seemed to have heard about it.

So the cancellations increased. They came over the phone and they came through the post. The hardest ones of all came on the very doorsteps, in notes stuffed into the empty bottles. They ranged from the cold politeness of *Regret no more milk required* to the very rude. (*We want cream on top the milk, not dead mice. Now shove off.* This was a mild one compared with some.)

Louie redoubled his efforts to catch the culprit at work. Instead of dashing around in circles, he dashed around in figures of eight and double threes and egg-and-darts and clover leaves and interlocking rings. Smitty and Tim hardly knew whether they were coming or going. It was no longer a simple milk *round.* It was a milk round-and-round-and-out-and-back-and-round-again, as Louie tried to nobble the nobbler.

But it was useless. The fixer seemed to have stopped altogether. No more real complaints came in that week. And, after all, why should the nobbler have gone on? The main damage had been done. Rumor was doing the rest, and you can't catch up with rumor even if you dash around so fast you catch up with yourself.

What's more, Smitty's theory about the kinds of objects that had been found (or were supposed to have been found) had also occurred to others besides Smitty. It had also occurred to the directors of New Day Dairies. Awkward questions were being asked by the Head Office. And although Louie was the best milkman in the country, and although he was probably a secret director himself, he began to get some pretty cool looks back at the dairy. Even Mr. Peters seemed to treat him pretty coolly now. Louie wasn't exactly in the doghouse. You couldn't say that. But he'd certainly been shoved out into the tool shed.

Black, then, it looked. And black it was.

And on the Saturday of that blackest of weeks— one week after the summons and just under a month before the case—there came the darkest news of all.

"I'm sorry," said Louie, scowling at the bluebirds on his arm, "but I'm having to lay you off. Both of you."

He was looking at the bluebirds. It might have sounded as if he was thinking of having the tattoo marks removed. As a sign of mourning maybe.

But he was speaking to Tim and Smitty.

Chapter 7

LOUIE'S ADVICE

Tim and Smitty looked shocked.

Tim and Smitty *were* shocked.

Getting a job with Louie's Lot was like joining
Government Service. It was like becoming a policeman or a tax collector. Getting picked by Louie
wasn't easy. There were the tests he gave you and
the two-week trial. But once you'd got through
those the job was permanent. So long as you didn't
make too many mistakes (three in any one month)
you were safe.

Well, neither Tim nor Smitty had made too many
mistakes. Louie had never got around to saying so
outright, but he even gave them the impression they
were very good. Above the average even for Louie's

Lot. Every boy he'd ever had seemed to get this impression—but that's beside the point. The point was that Tim and Smitty had not made too many mistakes. They'd done nothing wrong. Yet they were now getting fired.

"Both of us?" said Smitty, in a whisper.

His mother was Italian. She didn't know much English. She did most of her talking with her eyebrows, her eyes, her mouth-corners—twisting them up and down, this way and that. Smitty was falling back into his mother's ways now. His eyebrows shot up, crashed down. From the front, his mouth kept going into a U shape, upside down, ∩, very rapidly. From the side, his bottom lip kept jutting out, also very rapidly. His eyes rolled. He looked as if he was giving them a good rinse around in the tears that had started to form.

They were all sitting in the cab of the truck. They had just finished the morning route—what bit of it there was left. Louie had parked the truck just outside the dairy. He was staring straight ahead now. He looked as if he'd just seen a crack in the windshield.

"Yer—both of you," he grunted. He blew hard at his cigarette, and ash drifted like a shower of rain over his knees.

By now both Tim and Smitty saw how it was. It wasn't a question of making mistakes, of course. The route just wasn't big enough any more.

60

"Sid's having to lay his two off an' all," grunted Louie. "It's not just you."

Smitty's face looked as if it would never be the same again. Eyebrows, eyes, mouth, and now nose and ears were twitching away so furiously that it looked as if they'd never regain their proper places.

"Can't you—can't you just keep one of us?" asked Tim. "Smitty . . . He's been with you longest."

Louie looked as if he was going to spit his cigarette clean through the windshield. Smitty's features stopped jerking for a moment. They remained frozen, all in the wrong places.

Then Louie shook his head.

"Orders," he said. "There's not enough work for me and Sid. It'll be Sid next. Married man, an' all."

"Well—well, look—it can't go on like this forever," said Tim.

"Can't it?" grunted Louie.

"We'll be getting some of these customers back after a bit. You know what the Rely-On-Us milk's like."

Louie nodded. He uttered a word. It was a word that told Tim that he did indeed know what the Rely-On-Us milk was like.

"That could *do* with a few dead mice in it," he added. "Give it some body."

"Well, then," said Tim, "they'll be coming back to us. The route'll grow again."

"You're forgetting," said Louie, "the court case."

"What *about* it?" said Tim. "Everybody knows already. Everybody knows we've been summonsed."

"Yer," said Louie. "Only some of them don't believe it. Nearly every customer who's sticking with us thinks it's just another rumor. When they see it in the paper——"

Louie cracked his right hand down on the bluebirds. He gave them the hiding of their lives.

"Well, you never know," said Tim. "You can't be sure. And what I say is this. I say we stick with you. I say we stay on the route and do it for nothing. Till we see if things get any better. Eh, Smitty?"

Smitty nodded vigorously.

Louie said nothing for a while. He kept staring ahead, hissing quietly through his cigarette. He seemed to be very moved by Tim's offer. He *was* moved. But not exactly in the way the boys thought he was.

"Do it for *nothing!*" he said at last. "Do it for *nothing!*" he growled. "Is this all I've learned yer, all the time you been with me? Eh?" He had turned his head now. He was scowling at Tim as if the boy had suggested watering the cream. Smitty stirred, uneasy but much happier. It was beginning to sound like old times again. For a moment Smitty forgot about being laid off.

"Do it for *nothing!*" jeered Louie. "Amateurs!" he snarled. "Amateurs do things for nothing. An' I can't stand amateurs."

"But——"

"Amateurs work when they feel like it," went on Louie, really in his stride now, taking everything out on amateurs, all his troubles. "Amateurs do good work. Yer! Some of 'em. One or two. But only when they *feel like it*. An' what good yer gonner be to me after a week or two of *that*, eh? What good's amateur milk-boys on a real professional route? That's if we get it built up again which I don't think we will. Amateurs!"

By now, though, his voice had softened a little. He had turned to the windshield again.

"What you can do, to keep your hand in, is get hired by that Rely-On-Us mob. If they'll have you. *They're* not short of orders. Need as many new lads as they can get."

"Us?" cried Tim. "Work for *them?*"

Smitty's lip curled so much it was a wonder he didn't break his jaw.

Louie shrugged.

"Why not? A job's a job. At least yer'll be paid."

"But they're probably at the bottom of all this," said Tim. "You keep saying so yourself."

"Yer, but I can't prove it, can I?"

"No—only——"

"Only if I knew somebody who worked for them —somebody I could count on—somebody who'd keep their eyes an' ears open—well, then . . ."

Tim and Smitty stared at him.

Louie's own eyes were by no means wide open.

They had gone into slits. But through the up-curling cigarette smoke those slits were glittering keenly.

"You mean—if we—*us*—me and Smitty——"

"I mean you get around there now. Tell 'em yer've been fired. Tell 'em you're disgusted at the way you've been treated. They'll hire you. They'll hire you just to spite me. Not even countin' you've been *trained* by me. Then keep yer eyes an' ears open . . . Hey—and here . . . Here's an extra two weeks' pay . . ." Louie's cigarette gave a faint smile as he dipped into his back pocket. "Redundancy pay—the golden handshake."

But his face went very moody again as he waved away their thanks.

"Get goin'," he said. "While they've still got vacancies."

Chapter 8

THE TWO FACES
OF BERTIE WINKS

Bertie Winks, the head milkman of Rely-On-Us Dairies, was another dark man. Actually he was not quite so dark as Louie, but he was a lot dirtier and that evened things up a bit. It wasn't that he didn't shave regularly. He did. With an electric shaver while he was having his breakfast. It was just that he had more shaves than washes and this tended to show—especially in the cracks. Bertie's face had a lot of cracks.

His hair was black, with a dusty look about it. True, it was probably more trouble to keep clean than Louie's. Louie's was straight and flat and looked as if it would come up like new with just one wipe of a damp cloth. Bertie's was all tight curls, crimpy

all over, even at the back of his neck. It trapped the dust more—must have done—and that was probably why he used to wear a peaked cap.

This peaked cap is worth a minute on its own. It was navy blue and the peak was shiny. So were the silver letters at the front: RELY-ON-US. They were shiny too, mainly because they were made of a special metal that didn't need any cleaning. But the shiniest part of Bertie's cap was the big patch of grease on the top. When it was caught in certain lights it made Bertie look as if he'd got a halo. Just like the halo of an angel—which gave him a very odd look because he had the devil of a face.

It's tempting to go on about this cap of Bertie's

and leave out the face altogether. But duty is duty and if the reader can stand it the writer must.

That face . . .

Well . . .

It was a face that . . .

Look, Bertie Winks's face shouldn't have belonged to *anybody*—let alone a milkman. A milkman is often in touch with the public. He has to be. It's his job. What is more, he's in touch with the public mainly when they've just waked up. It's downright unfair that a busy housewife—with a hard day's work in front of her and maybe a hard night's dreams behind her—should have to set eyes on a face like Bertie's so early.

Mind you, Bertie himself tended to cut down the chances of this happening too often. Louie was a front-line milkman—or at least a front-*doorstep* milkman. Bertie was an armchair milkman—or at least a *driving-seat* milkman. Where Louie was always out and about with the lads, Bertie tended to sit back in the truck, reading over the horse-racing charts. But more about that later. We've still got to face that face.

Wellthenitwashorribleterriblemurderitwaslike . . .

Saying it quickly doesn't help, either. Let's not panic over this. Let's take it a bit at a time.

THE SKIN—muddy yellow.

THE NOSE—short but sharp, and it was always bright red around the nostrils. There was a reason for that. No—not drink. Bertie didn't take strong drink. He didn't smoke, either. The reason for this bright red around the nostrils—the only touch of color in his muddy yellow face—was . . . But that's something else we'll be coming to later.

THE EYES—one brown, one pale blue. This is really inside information, because the brown one he kept three-quarters shut most of the time. It was the pale blue one that people saw most of. It bulged a lot, especially at the ladies. This made it seem as if they were both pale blue.

THE TEETH—very small, of a curious, rather pretty shade of brown, set in a lot of gum.

THE CRACKS—noted above. Mainly across the forehead, down between the eyes, and deep down at either side of the mouth.

But THE MOUTH itself was the most nerve-jarring thing—quite apart from the teeth. It was the way he twisted it when he smiled. Up it slid on one side, toward the sleepy brown eye. And down it dipped at the other, away from the popping pale blue one. To those on the brown side this gave him the appearance of smiling—which was fair enough (though it was smiling in a nasty sort of way). To those on the pale blue side it gave him the appearance of scowling.

The pale blue scowling side was the left, where his unfortunate boys used to sit in the cab (for this was in England, remember). The smiling brown side was the public side.

Gilbert Dabbit seemed only ever to have seen him

on the smiling side. The Health Inspector seemed to think Bertie Winks was a model for all milkmen. But probably this had more to do with the peaked cap and the gray smock Bertie always wore on the route. *That* was what Gilbert Dabbit liked to see. If the Health Inspector had had his way it would have been the law of the land. All milkmen in smocks. All milkmen's heads in peaked caps. Neater. Tidier. Cleaner. Not like Louie in his old faded blue sweater, summer and winter alike.

But Louie's old blue sweater was faded through lots of washing.

And Bertie's smock was gray because that color didn't show the dirt.

Yet Louie smoked too much, the Health Inspector would probably have pointed out—if you'd argued with him. And Bertie Winks didn't smoke at all.

"Ah no!" you could have replied to that (if you'd known the facts). "But there are dirtier habits than smoking."

Which is true enough. Bertie Winks had one. He was fond of picking his nose. That's why his nostrils were always that bright red color.

No. Seen from a distance, Bertie might have looked the better milkman. With his cap (which Louie couldn't stand to see) and his smock, Bertie Winks might have seemed more capable of delivering milk. But looks aren't everything, as any detective will tell you. And the plain fact was that as a milkman Louie could *lose* Bertie Winks.

The milk-boys knew it. That was why there was always a big crowd of applicants whenever Louie had a vacancy. And that was why Bertie was always advertising for boys. That was why he couldn't keep them for longer than a month at a time.

The customers knew it. That was why (before this load of trouble) the New Day Dairy always had four times as many as the Rely-On-Us Dairy.

And Bertie Winks knew it.

That was why he hated Louie even more than Mr. Dabbit did. That was why the brown-eyed side of his face had hardly ever stopped smiling, from the day Louie's troubles had started.

It was smiling now, when Tim and Smitty came to ask about the vacancies. . . .

Chapter 9

BERTIE'S FINEST HOUR

The brown-eyed side of Bertie Winks's face wasn't smiling at Tim and Smitty, though. It wasn't smiling with joy at seeing *them*. In fact, Bertie had his back turned to Tim and Smitty when they entered the Rely-On-Us yard. He was doing something to the door of his shed.

The setup at Rely-On-Us was very like that at New Day Dairies. There was the parking lot with its cars and trucks lined up. There was the main building with its offices and tubs of flowers at one end and the bottling plant at the other. There was the long loading platform in front of the bottling plant, still wet from its hosing down. There were the jets and puffs of escaping steam and the usual rattle of bottles. And there were several sheds, dotted about the main yard.

One of these sheds was the head milkman's. No doubt Bertie could have had an office in the main block if he'd wanted. No doubt the Rely-On-Us manager was always offering him an office in the block, just as the New Day manager was always offering Louie one. But head milkmen are odd fellows. In most things they may be as much unlike one another as Bertie and Louie were. Yet they still feel the same way about sheds and offices. They're like outside dogs. Yard dogs. They seem to *need* something separate.

Anyway, that was where Bertie was when Tim and Smitty entered the yard. Doing something to the door of his shed. His cap was tilted back, the greasy patch shining gloriously in the midmorning sun. And as they got nearer, approaching at an angle to the right of him, they saw he was smiling. He was smiling so broadly that that side of his mouth was somewhere up by his right eye. It had shot so far up that it had become blended with one of the cracks.

Then they saw why. Bertie Winks was painting. He'd been writing something in yellow paint. On the door of the shed there had always been this sign, which he'd also painted himself:

B. WINKS

HEAD MILMAN

(Either the slob couldn't spell or, as usual, he'd been cutting down on work. Those are just two reasons for the missing K.) And now, as Tim and Smitty approached, he was just putting the finishing touches to an extra line he'd been painting. This line squeezed between B. WINKS and HEAD MILMAN read: ASS MANAGER AND

So the whole sign now added up to:

B. WINKS

ASS MANAGER AND

HEAD MILMAN

Tim coughed.

Bertie jumped.

He must have been very wrapped up in his work. He jumped so hard it made the brush slip and mess up the last extra word. Now the sign looked more like:

B. WINKS

ASS MANAGER ASS

HEAD MILMAN

Bertie was annoyed.

He spun around and gave them the pale blue side of his face, full blast.

"What the——"

Then he stopped. When he saw who it was, even the pale blue eye began to close.

"What do *you* want?" he growled.

Bertie Winks knew who Tim and Smitty were, of course.

Suspicion was written all over his face. Some of it in yellow paint.

Smitty tried to make a bit of polite chat.

"Goin' over to donkeys, then, Bertie? Goin' back to donkeys and carts?"

"How jer mean?" growled Bertie.

"Making you manager of the asses. Ass manager."

This was the wrong line. Smitty had never been the boy for tact. Tim gave him a nudge to tell him to keep quiet. It was more important than ever now that they should keep on the right side of Bertie. They looked as if they were on to something here, all right. If Louie was the world's best milkman Bertie was the world's worst. Yet it looked as if he'd been promoted. Why?

"Don't be stupid, Smitty," said Tim, before Bertie had got far with his reply. "That ASS stands for ASSISTANT. They must have promoted Bertie to assistant manager. Congratulations, Bertie!"

Bertie's brown side gave a jerk. But he still looked suspicious.

"What jer want?" he repeated.

"Jobs," said Smitty.

"On the route," said Tim.

"With Rely-On-Us," said Smitty.

Bertie was now looking much better. He gave his nose a gentle picking.

"What's wrong with working for Louie?" he asked, leering.

"*That* rat!" said Tim. (They'd worked out before-hand what they were going to say.)

"He's fired us," said Smitty. "A minute's notice!"

"Without warning," added Tim.

"The creep!" said Smitty.

"The big lousy jerk!" said Tim.

"Never did trust him," said Smitty.

"A crumb if ever there was one," said Tim.

"A long wet streak!" said Smitty.

(Although they'd made it up to call Louie all these names—simply to put Bertie off his guard—they found they were enjoying themselves. After all, Louie *had* been pretty strict at times. He *was* a pretty hard man. He *had* said a few hard things to them in their time. So it was nice to let off steam like this. Especially as they knew Louie himself would have had to approve.)

"An all-time jerk," said Tim.

"A world-class jerk," said Smitty.

"A real top jerk," said Tim.

"A jerk of jerks," said Smitty.

"All right! All right!" said Bertie. This had been music to his ears. He'd picked his nose till it glowed. But he wanted to get down to business. "I'm glad folk are coming round to my way of thinking after all these years. Come into the office and we'll see what we can do."

Office!

The outdoor toilet in a neglected roadside picnic area had a better right to the name of office than *that* shack.

The only furniture was a table and a bus seat. At least that's what Tim judged these articles to be. The table might only have been a few planks slung across a couple of trestles. There was so much rubbish on the top it was hard to tell. It might even have been an upturned packing case, for you couldn't see the legs. Tacked across the front was what looked like four old coal sacks, stitched together. To keep the draft off Bertie's legs, no doubt. Come to that it might have been made *entirely* of rubbish. Layer upon layer of rubbish rising from the floor to a height of two foot six.

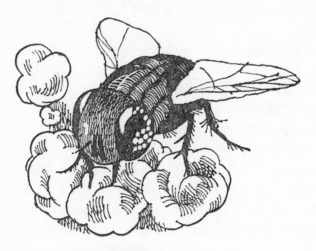

The top layer, anyway, contained:

several scattered order books;
one ready reckoner;

a racing form guide;

three *Daily Mirrors,* folded at racing page;

two mugs, both with black cracks, brown chipped edges, and tea dregs (one lot with gray-green spots of floating mold);

one dull spoon tied to one of the mug handles with damp brown string;

one crumpled ball of paper, brown and white, spotted with hamburger grease;

about half a pack of cards, scattered, with *two* aces of spades;

four bottles, all three-quarters full of milk, two lots of which had curdled (Bertie liked only cream in his tea); and

a telephone, once black and shiny, now furry gray and looking like a fly hive.

Tim judged that the seat (on which Bertie now sat down) had been a bus seat because of its shape. The pattern had long since got lost under the grease and grime. It looked as if it had come from a bus that had done twenty years' service in a rough part of a coal-mining town. Then another twenty on hire to a building firm.

As for the rest of the shack, three pairs of rubber boots were scattered in various corners—one pair saying its prayers. On one wall there hung some oilskins. Another wall was papered with pin-ups. (This was the one on Bertie's pale blue pop-eyed side.)

The top layer of rubbish began to stir. Bertie had

put his feet up on the desk. They sank several inches into the junk. A bluebottle fly, angry at being disturbed, flew out of the phone's mouthpiece.

"So you want to work for us, eh?"

Bertie took off his cap and hung it on one of the milk bottles. The bluebottle became interested in the patch of grease. Then Bertie took out of his breast pocket one of the biggest pairs of glasses Tim and Smitty had ever seen. Brand-new, they looked— with thick black frames. He put them on. You could tell he fancied himself in them. Bertie Winks, head milkman, gave place to B. Winks, assistant manager. It was the removal of the cap that did it. And the putting on of the glasses. Executive-type.

Bertie leaned back. He gave them the pale blue side of his face. With those glasses wrapped around the top of it, it was a terrible sight to see.

"Well, you'll have to waken your ideas up if you do," said Bertie. He snatched off his glasses and gave one of the sidepieces such a slap it made Tim jump and Smitty go pale. Then Bertie got to work nibbling the end of one of the sidepieces, like a rat at a fat stick of licorice. "Yer," sneered Bertie, finally taking the sidepiece out of his mouth and giving his nose a poke with it. "You'll have to smarten yourselves up. We got a reputation to keep."

He put the glasses back on. Then he held them a little way from his nose, the way he'd seen some of the tough talkers do it on TV. He held them there as he stared hard at Tim and Smitty.

Actually he was delighted, of course. Overjoyed. This was Bertie's finest hour. Tim and Smitty coming begging for a job topped it off beautifully.

First—no doubt about it—Rely-On-Us Dairies were very short-staffed.

Second—they had long since run out of all possible boys: the sorts of slobs and dopes who'd even think of working for Bertie.

Third—this was the topping off, this made his joy complete—not only had he lived to see Louie's business fall off. Not only had he lived to see Louie in the doghouse at New Day Dairies. Not only had these old dreams come true. But here he was, actually on the point of taking over two of Louie's best lads.

But he tried not to show it.

"When could you start?" he asked, with his sharp little nose in the air.

Not "When *can* you start?" note. "When *could* you start?"

Tim and Smitty were both feeling sick. It cost Tim much to stammer out his answer.

"To-tomorrow . . ."

"All right, then." Bertie snatched and slapped his glasses again. Again he gave his nose a poking with the end of the sidepiece." You can go round with me. I'll see what yer made of." He put his glasses back on again with a *very* ugly leer. "Be here at half-past six. An' see you're not late. We believe in being punctual *here*. Deliveries on the dot."

Both Tim and Smitty felt like doing some delivering on the dot just then. But a different sort of delivery from what Bertie meant. On a different sort of dot.

For they knew all about *Bertie's* punctuality. Where Louie always started alone, at 4:30, Bertie rarely made a move till it was going on seven. His boys were always having to hang about waiting for him. And then having to break their necks nearly, trying to catch up on their deliveries. You ought to have heard Louie on the subject of Bertie's punctuality!

Bertie was giving them the tough TV look now. With a good wash and shave, much plastic surgery, a good barber, and a clean shirt, he might have made the Huntley-Brinkley show just at that moment.

"Well . . . shove off, then," he said. "I got my paperwork to do." He glanced at the racing page of the latest of the *Daily Mirrors*. "You'd better go and get some rest. If you're gonner work for me you'll need to be alert. Not like for that layabout you been riding round with up to now."

Smitty hesitated. Tim thought his grip had snapped and he was going to tell Bertie a few of the facts of life. But no. A plot was a plot, but with Smitty business was also business.

"Er—the pay," he said. "How much?"

Bertie considered this. What he did with those glasses in the next two minutes it would have taken a computer to keep track of. Then he named his figure. The boys were shocked.

They hadn't hoped to get as much as they had with Louie. Louie always paid five shillings more than anyone else, once he was satisfied with a boy. But they hadn't been ready for *this*.

"*Mamma mia!* That's fifteen shillings less than Louie paid us!" gasped Smitty.

Bertie's sidepiece nearly got jammed up his nose, he gave such a snigger at that.

"Yer! But it's a sight more than he's giving you *now*, isn't it? Take it or leave it."

Tim and Smitty sighed. It was in a good cause, sure enough. The main thing was that they were being hired. And, after all, it was even better than they'd hoped. Bertie might have put them on with one of the other Rely-On-Us milkmen. But no— they were going on with him. And if anyone at Rely-On-Us had nobbled Louie it was likely to be Bertie Winks. So they were off to a flying start.

But it was hard, even so. Very hard.

Smitty's mouth began to look as if he'd got something stuck in his teeth.

"O.K.," said Tim, brave as they come. "We'll take it."

And plucking Smitty's sleeve, he steered his pal out of the shack before the words that boy wanted to utter could find their way out of his face.

Chapter 10

KING OF THE SLOBS

"How you find Bertie, then?" asked Louie, when they went around to tell him.

Louie was in his own shack.

It wasn't exactly as clean and shining as a dentist's office, itself. It wasn't much bigger than Bertie's. But the boys now knew what a spider feels like when it crawls out of a grease trap into the sink.

The table was a table. You could see that at once. There were spaces on top to prove it, between the neat piles of order books and leaflets and weekly return forms. And the seat behind it was a stool. There was no puzzling over that.

The floor was bare, right enough. And it had rather more cigarette butts scattered about it, crushed and flattened, than Gilbert Dabbit would have liked. But they were very *small* cigarette butts. They always were when Louie had finished with them. And the ash and the scorch marks gave the bare boards an interesting look, almost like a pattern. Anyway, you don't sit on the floor.

One wall was, oddly enough, just like Bertie's. That was where the oilskins were hanging. But it is hard for anyone to get oilskins to hang tidily like curtains, and the boys hadn't held that against Bertie. The opposite wall, though, was completely different from the other milkman's. The only pin-ups on this wall of Louie's were:

one large-scale map of the district;
a list of customers' telephone numbers; and
a list headed *Regular Specials*.

The large-scale map had been marked off into routes: Louie's and Sid's. Usually it had little red flags dotted about on it. These were made out of pins and bits of red bottle caps. They were stuck in to show Louie at a glance where business wasn't so good. Streets where fewer than half the houses took New Day milk. Then he would know where to keep his eyes open for new customers.

There were never many of these red flags as a rule. Now there was none. This didn't mean business was good everywhere though. Just the opposite. It meant that business was so bad all over town that it wasn't worth sticking any flags in at all.

The list of customers' telephone numbers was another sign of Louie's efficiency. If ever the grocery department had any special offers, Louie would do a bit of calling around. If the old pensioner who supplied him with vegetables and flowers had anything special, Louie would do a bit of calling around then. And so on. It made these customers feel good to be called like this. It made them say what a pity they didn't get service like this everywhere. But now—even some of them had deserted him. Louie had marked these off with little crosses.

The list headed *Regular Specials* gave the names and addresses of all the customers who gave special orders at regular times. There were some who had extra pints every Saturday and Sunday. There were some who went away every weekend and didn't want any at all then. There was a young couple who had a rich old uncle to tea on the third Sunday of every month—one large heavy cream. There was an old lady who gave her cat a treat on its birthday. Because cats don't live as long as humans she let it have a birthday every month. The 20th. One small light cream.

Most of these people thought Louie was a mind reader. Even when they forgot to order one of their specials, there it would be. On the doorstep. On the dot. Marvelous. It just shows what human nature's like—and how bad Louie's trouble was—when I say that eight of *them* had deserted him. The rats!

But Louie had asked a question.

"How you find Bertie, then?"

"Dirty!" said Smitty, quick as a flash.

And Louie laughed.

"Ho!" he went.

One short shout, sprinkling them with ash.

Then he dusted down his bluebirds and said, in his normal growl, with his normal moody look:

"Dirty Bertie! That's a good 'un!"

It was the first time Tim had ever known Louie to laugh, actually to laugh out loud. He was glad he hadn't been blinking when it happened. Otherwise he might have missed it.

Louie quickly got back to business.

"He's been promoted, eh?"

"Yes," said Smitty. "Ass manager."

Just like Smitty. Proud of having been the first person in living memory to make Louie laugh, he was trying it again. This time all he got was a gloomy frown.

"Well, that's a start," murmured Louie. "I mean we know he didn't get it for smartness."

Tim agreed.

"That's what makes us sure he's at the back of all this nobbling."

Louie gave him a look that could have punched home a six-inch nail.

"I was sure without that, mate! All *I* want is proof." He gave the bluebirds a crisp chop with the side of his spare hand. "Stick to him. See who he talks to. Apart from customers, I mean—allus chatting up the young birds, Bertie. I don't mean them. I mean anyone else. Mates of his he might start braggin' to. And partic'ly anyone he might have got to do the dirty work for him. He won't have dared to do it hisself . . . O.K.?"

They nodded.

"Right!" said Louie. "Well, now you'd better blow. From now on don't let anyone see you hanging round here. You're in Bertie's Mob now. Only if you get something definite come around here. Then it won't matter. Once I get me hands on something definite I'll smash him. Then it'll be back to business as usual . . . O.K.?"

The mention of business reminded Smitty. He told Louie of the lousy wages Bertie had offered.

Louie nodded.

"Not surprised," he growled. "What'll surprise me is if you get even *that* much, end the week."

"Eh? Why?"

"Got a bad memory for figures, Bertie. The adding-up kind, that is. You'll see . . . Anyway, sooner you find something definite, sooner you're back in the old Welfare State here . . . Now blow. I got some addresses to be looking up."

The next few days were the most depressing that Tim and Smitty had ever spent in their lives. They were interesting days, yes. They were even at times exciting days, true. But depressing, depressing— very depressing.

It wasn't as if they hadn't known what to expect. It wasn't as if they hadn't been warned.

They knew about Bertie's lateness. They knew about Bertie's laziness—picking his nose and the winners while the boys rushed around to catch up. And they knew about Bertie's slovenliness with things like stacking.

His stacking especially.

Halfway through the route on any day you could easily have mistaken his truck for a scrap-metal man's. Crates used to be piled up on the back at all angles. Empties got stuffed in with fulls. Some fulls rolled about loose. Some crates full of fulls would get buried under the rest. This meant Bertie always left a trail: (*a*) of milk that leaked out of the loose rolling fulls, (*b*) of the crates themselves.

Yes, crates. Because he never kept up with his stacking, it meant he'd less room on the truck than he should have had. And this meant he'd got to keep dumping empty crates in little piles at street corners and on bits of spare land.

"Pick 'em up later," he used to say—but he never caught up with them all. Bertie's littered crates made good stumps for bowling at in games of street cricket. Roughneck boys liked them for the nice big crash they made when chucked into someone's back yard. Burglars found them handy as steps, when climbing over walls. Little girls played house with them. Louie could go on for half an hour at a time, telling you about Bertie's dumped crates and their uses. "Anything 'cept what they was made for!" he used to grunt.

The boys knew about things like that and expected them. And Louie had warned them about Bertie's habit of chatting with the young wives. But what they *didn't* expect were things like:

the missing out of customers and sometimes whole streets;
the unbelievable sloppiness of Bertie's delivery when he did get out of the cab; and
the *length* of some of those chats.

"That's the fifth cup of tea he's gone in someone's house for!"

"Yer—and they're all young birds, *amico*. Just like Louie said."

"Don't know how they stick him—face like that."

"It's the extra cream he gives 'em on the side—that's what *that* is, mate! Been watching him. Slips a jar in his pocket every time he goes to chat 'em up."

Tim and Smitty soon got tired of making observations like this. They soon got tired of making calculations, too, about how long Bertie could go on snitching cream for his lady friends without the dairy finding out. Besides, there wasn't much time. The later Bertie was in starting, and the longer he took over his cups of tea, the less time was left for delivery. And since Bertie himself did nothing to make up for lost time, the boys were run off their feet.

They did their best. Although it was only Bertie they were working for, Louie's training told. It *hurt* those boys to see a milk route in a mess—even Bertie's. So they did their best at least to see that the customers didn't suffer.

But it was hopeless.

"I mean what can we do with a book like this?" groaned Smitty, more than once. "*Look* at it! Just *look* at it! *Impossibile!*"

And he'd wave the tattered order book that looked as if rats had been at it—full of crossings-out, grease spots, blots, stale crumbs, damp fluff, and fingernail clippings.

"Months out of date as well!" Tim would add—having tried to do some checking on the first morning. "He's not even bothered to put in the new ones—the ones he pinched off New Day."

But Bertie didn't worry.

"Don't come pesterin' me about *that!*" he'd say, taking a finger out of his nose to wave them away. "Knock and ask if you're not sure."

Or: "Leave two at every house down there an' let 'em sort it out between 'em."

That would be early in the route. Later, when even Bertie could see they were getting pushed for time, he'd get reckless.

"Aw, never mind that end 'un today! What they want to live right at the end for? Serve 'em right!"

Or: "Sorry, Walker Street!" he might sing out, passing the place without even slackening speed. "Yer'll have to come to the dairy for it today. It's near enough!"

As for the few dozen bottles Bertie actually did put himself out to deliver personally—at houses where there weren't any friendly young wives— Tim and Smitty could only gape with horror.

For Bertie didn't believe in bending his back more than he could help. So the bottles used to land on the doorstep with a crash.

And, for the same reason, Bertie didn't believe in doing with his hands what he could do with his feet more easily. So those bottles that fell on their sides were hoiked up with the side of his boot.

And Bertie didn't believe in going against nature's will. So if he didn't hoik a bottle upright with his boot at the first go, he'd let it lie.

The result of all this was a pool on nearly every doorstep he delivered at. The clue Louie found in the pool on Mrs. Bellamy's doorstep wouldn't have been a clue at all for Bertie. It wouldn't have been unusual enough.

Empties Bertie ignored. Milk notes in bottles he never bothered with. Crates could look after themselves. Customers—who did they think they *were*, anyway? That was Bertie's outlook.

In fact, if the BBC or CBS were to have run a Slob of the Year contest, the title would have been in Bertie's murky pocket right from Heat One. None of the usual slobs would have stood a chance. Not even the old witches British Railways get to throw cups of tea across counters at customers. Not even the house painters who slap it on over the cobwebs. Not even the window cleaners who wait till the water in their buckets cakes like mud. Slob waiters, slob bus drivers, slob policemen, slob teachers, slob butchers, slob bakers, slob writers, slob critics, slob lawyers, slob parsons, slob politicians, slob pop singers, slob doctors, slob actors, slob football players, slob referees, slob boxers, slob wrestlers: of all slobs everywhere, Bertie Winks was King.

But, of course, the boys weren't there to report on Bertie's slobbishness. They were there to watch carefully. They were there to note who he chatted to besides young wives. And at first they didn't seem to have much luck.

There was a policeman he had a few words with, and these words were: "Yes, officer! Certainly, officer! Sorry, officer! Nice day, isn't it?"

That was when he'd parked on the wrong side of High Street.

There were the garbage collectors he had a few words with, and these were: "Back a bit, back a bit, now straighten up. Right."

There were one or two people he waved at from the cab. One morning he even had a word with Gilbert Dabbit, near the City Hall. There they were, tearing along the road, late as usual, when suddenly Bertie grunted and slowed down.

"Good morning, Mr. Dabbit! Nice now, isn't it?" he crooned, leaning out of the cab and transferring to the peak of his cap the finger that had been up his nose. "Did you use that stuff on your roses I was tellin' you about? Aw, splendit! *Splen*dit, Mr. Dabbit!"

Smitty made a throwing-up face at this, and Tim didn't feel too good, either. But there was nothing unusual about Bertie's sucking up to the Health Inspector, really. There was nothing any more unusual about that than there was about the other brief chats already mentioned. Naturally, the boys didn't expect him to say anything out loud about nobbling Louie's milk even if he should have met someone in the know. In fact, what they were looking for mainly was regularity. Did he *regularly* have a friendly chat with anyone he met on the route? Another early-morning deliverer, perhaps, like a mailman or paper boy? Someone likely to be in a position to do the nobbling for him?

But the only early-morning deliverer he had a regular brief chat with seemed to be Louie himself. And that was far from friendly, anyway.

"Still plodding on then, Louie, eh?" he'd call out.

Or: "When you've run out of customers come and have a word with us. We'll hire you. Sweepin' the yard!"

Or: "See who I've got workin' with me now? They're a bit slow. They got some bad habits. But I'm licking 'em into shape!"

Only to this last remark did Louie bother to reply. Flicking Tim and Smitty with a look that stung, he said:

"You can have 'em. Never was any good. Just your sort!"

Louie was kidding, of course. He must have been. It was all part of the plot. All the same, that look he gave them stung, and his words rubbed salt in. For the rest of that route they delighted the leering Bertie with another string of comments about Louie. They, too, were kidding, of course. They, too, were only acting. But it was acting with feeling, and Louie's ears must have burned as brightly as his cigarette.

That was on Wednesday, by the way.

It was on Thursday—just when they were thinking they'd been wasting their time—that they made *real* progress.

Chapter 11

A BOY CALLED KELLY

It happened while Tim and Smitty were busy delivering. Bertie, as usual, was back in the truck.

Bertie had a lot of paperwork to get through that morning. There were no fewer than five race meetings being held later in the day. So, to make sure he could settle down and do the job properly, he had cut down the number of stops.

"All this stoppin' and startin' breaks me concentration," he had said, early on. "I'll never get past the 2:30 at Doncaster at this rate."

So he had cut down the number of stops—halved them, in fact. This meant that Tim and Smitty had to do twice as much walking. They had to cover twice the usual distance and that was quite a way, because Bertie never had been lavish with his stops. They hadn't liked this at first, of course. They'd done so much grumbling that if Bertie's picking hadn't been keeping all his spare blood busy around his nostrils, *he'd* have had a pair of red ears too.

But before the morning was out, they were very glad about this extra distance they had to cover.

It meant that anyone who wanted a quiet word with Bertie would feel easier about going up to him.

It meant that anyone who wanted to discuss a bit of dirty work with Bertie without being overheard or even seen—well, he'd feel he'd got a good chance.

With Bertie in the truck, bent over the problem of whether to concentrate on second favorites or go strictly by form, and the boys two streets away, bent under the extra weight of bottles—the time would seem ripe for anyone who wanted a quiet word with the milkman.

And there was such a one. Oh yes indeed, there was such a one!

For days he'd been lurking around, waiting for a chance to speak to Bertie on his own. *And* about a bit of dirty work too. In fact there had been times when Bertie had seen him out of the corner of his three-quarter-closed brown eye. Bertie had actually seen him and turned away, fast, making signs that said: "Blow, you fool! Get lost! Don't come near me with these two here! What you thinking of, you fool? Go on! Get lost! Try later (if yer can catch me—heh! heh!)—not now. Anyway, what you want to see me about? Everything's settled, en' it? Course it is! So get lost!"

And the signs he made to say all this were very simple. A circular motion of the wrist. A flicking motion with his nose finger. A jerking motion of the elbow. A twitching motion of the cheek. A wagging motion of the tongue. A nibbling motion of the small brown teeth. And one full spit out upon the pavement.

But today he'd no excuse. There he was, alone in the truck, with a faint clinking in the distance that said the boys were a good three streets away. And today he was so busy with his paperwork that he didn't even see this Other approaching.

"Boo!" grunted the newcomer, stopping his bike and resting an arm against Bertie's door.

"Krywhoopercash!" gasped Bertie, jumping so violently he nearly crushed his cap against the roof.

"I want a word with you," said the newcomer . . .

Meanwhile, Tim had found he'd run short of cream. Two extra bottles were needed, and two angry housewives had been there to remind him. Sighing gently—for this was nothing unusual on the King of the Slob's route—Tim had turned back. On Louie's route he would have run all the way if such a thing had happened. But then, on Louie's route such things so rarely did happen.

Walking then, and asking himself why he should break his neck for Bertie, he approached the truck.

Now note this. The newcomer had approached by bike, on the driver's side. Tim was approaching on foot, on the near side.

Note this further. The newcomer had approached on soft rubber tires, while Bertie had been deep in study. Tim was approaching on soft rubber soles.

He wasn't approaching quite so silently as the newcomer had done, because up to then he hadn't seen any need to. And Bertie, of course, was no longer deep in study. But it was just as effective really, for by then Bertie and the newcomer were so deep in *argument* that they'd never have heard if a battalion of Marines had come marching up.

"Garn! Get lost! What d'yer take me for, mate? Think I'm made er money?" Bertie was squealing.

At first Tim thought that Bertie must have gone mad and was rowing with himself—blue-eyed side versus the brown. Then, peering through the mess of muddled crates and empties and fulls, he caught sight of a bicycle saddle, a bending gray-flanneled bottom, a strip of blue blazer, and part of a canvas newspaper bag.

"I don't care!" a voice was saying—and Tim blinked, trying to remember where he'd heard it before. "You promised me another quid when the job was finished. Another pound, Winks. Another twenty shillings."

"But it *ain't* finished yet, yer wet!" yelped Bertie.

"I keep tellin' yer! It ain't finished till next month. The tenth."

This was a date engraved in deep black letters on the heart of everyone connected with New Day Dairies. Tim held his breath.

"Yes, but it's as good as!" the voice was saying—and now Tim blinked again. He'd recognized it. "You know as well as I do that it's as good as, Winks. Come on—that other quid!"

There came a soft sound, as of the flicking of fingers. It was mingled with another soft sound, as of gargling. Bertie sounded on the brink of a fit.

"Gah!" he got out at last. "Goh! Huh! And anyway, mate—what sort of job you call *that*? I been meaning to tell yer. Overdoin' it like that. I mean —that goldfish! Yer fool! I told you to stick to things like shoestrings an' that. Bandages. And clock parts to make it look——"

"If I don't get that other quid *now,* I'll go straight round and see the Public Health feller——"

"What? And tell 'em it was you who shoved the things in while you was doing yer papers?"

"Yes. And tell them it was you who told me, *hired* me, gave me money to do it. Me, only a kid, a juvenile. You, a grown man. *Part* of the money, anyway. Come on . . ."

More finger flicking.

"Well—well, look. Be sensible. Don't be stupid. Don't start kickin' up here. Yer'll have them kids hearing us. They'll be back any minute. Tell yer what. I'll give you ten shillings of it now and the rest after the case."

"You'd *better!*"

"Yes, well—eh?"

All at once Tim realized he must have been heard. Or maybe it was Smitty, coming up the street, clinking his empties.

Tim tried to look as if he'd only just arrived. He started fumbling about in the mess for the extra creams. He heard the truck door open and Bertie get out.

Tim picked out the two cream bottles. Bertie's footsteps came flapping behind him. There also came the tick-ticking of bicycle wheels. Smitty's clinking also came nearer.

"Oh, it's you!"

Bertie sounded very suspicious.

Tim looked up, smiling brightly.

"Hello!" he said. "Hello!"

The first hello was for Bertie. The second hello was for the boy with the bike, who had come around behind Bertie.

"Extra cream," Tim continued. "Lady down there . . . There's a paper boy behind you." He added this last remark to try to make it sound as if he'd only just arrived. As if he'd only just noticed the paper boy. As if he thought the paper boy had only just arrived too.

The paper boy was called Kelly.

He was a tall boy with sandy hair in a fringe. He was a high school senior.

Size, hair, school, job—these things Tim knew by just looking at him.

The name Kelly he knew from past experience.

When Tim had applied to join Louie's Lot, this Kelly had applied too. Tim had passed Louie's tests using brains and energy. Kelly had tried to pass them using brains and guile. Tim had got the job. Kelly hadn't. Tim had been glad. Kelly had been mad.

Kelly had been so mad he'd tried to get Tim into trouble with Louie. He'd tried so hard he'd nearly succeeded. He'd tried so very hard he'd nearly got Smitty into trouble too. He——

But that's another story. Just now he was looking at Tim as suspiciously as Bertie was. His eyes were narrow as he stared at Tim. That made three narrow eyes altogether plus one popping pale blue one. They'd got Tim covered.

"Hello"—clink!—"hello, hello—what *you* want?"

This was Smitty, all unsuspecting, just arrived, looking his old enemy Kelly up and down. Ready for a bit of back talk any day, Smitty.

Nobody took any notice of him.

Bertie and Kelly were still trying to figure out whether Tim had heard anything. Tim was still trying to look as if he hadn't—juggling the cream bottles about, smiling, sniffing.

"Well, don't just stand there!" grunted Bertie in

the end. "Get 'em delivered if somebody's waiting for 'em!"

That showed he was rattled. Bertie Winks worried about keeping a customer waiting!

Then Bertie turned to Kelly.

"Yes, I'll have an *Express* if you got one to spare," he said, as if that was all they'd been talking about.

Bertie was very thoughtful on the rest of the route. He hardly said a word. And though he still kept on studying his papers, his heart wasn't in it, Tim and Smitty could tell.

"Think he's wise to you?" asked Smitty, after Tim had told him what he'd heard. This was while they were away from the truck, delivering. "Think he know's *you're* wise to *him?*"

"I don't know," murmured Tim. He wasn't all that worried really. He could hardly wait for the route to be finished now. He could hardly wait to go straight around to New Day Dairies and tell of what he'd heard. "Course, it'll be better if he hasn't. But he *has* gone quiet."

Bertie had indeed gone quiet. Toward the end of the route he'd even given up pretending to study his horses. Instead he just sat in the cab, picking away and staring thoughtfully at nothing with his pale blue eye.

Whatever he had been thinking, he must have made up his mind by the time they got back to the dairy yard and into his shack. He must have made up his mind either:

(*a*) that having Tim and Smitty with him was too big a risk anyway; or

(*b*) that he'd shock Tim into blurting out the truth.

For, as soon as he'd got settled in behind his junk heap of a desk, and put his feet up, and taken his cap off, and put his glasses on, and blown a kiss to his pet bluebottle, he said something that might have fitted either (*a*) or (*b*).

He said, looking Tim straight in the chest:

"You're fired."

Tim blinked. He *nearly* blurted it out. He *nearly* said: "So what, you slob! I've found out what I wanted."

But a little voice seemed to tell him not to give anything away—to keep Bertie guessing as much as possible. A little hard voice, it was, that seemed to come from behind a fiercely glowing, crisply wagging cigarette.

So all he said was:

"Oh? Why?"

"Becost yer not good enough. Not alert enough. Too slow. Too sloppy. Too——"

"You *what?*"

Smitty sounded as if *he* might blurt it out. He sounded as if *he* might not have heard that little voice. Tim stepped back a pace. Onto Smitty's left toes. Gentle but firm.

"If that's the way you feel," Tim said to Bertie, "you'd better pay me up."

"That's the way I feel," said Bertie. "Here y'are."

He tossed a coin onto the junk, just in front of Tim.

Tim stared at it.

"Two shillings? But this is Thursday! It's nearly a week and——"

"Take it or leave it," sniffed Bertie, giving his glasses the tough talker's tug. "That's all you been worth."

Once again Tim nearly blurted out what he knew. He opened his mouth, ready. But luckily Smitty beat him to the blurt. And that boy was so mad that what *he* blurted had nothing to do with newspaper boys or Health Inspectors or sabotaging other milkmen's milk. What Smitty blurted was more basic than that. What Smitty blurted—all mixed up with snatches of Italian that sounded terribly violent and profane—was all about:

Bertie's meanness;
Bertie's ancestors;
Bertie's parents;
Bertie's appearance (in general);
Bertie's left eye;
Bertie's right eye;
Bertie's nose;
Bertie's nostrils;
Bertie's mouth;
Bertie's teeth;
Bertie's cap;
Bertie's smock;
Bertie's glasses (for which he suggested some very odd uses);
Bertie's office;
Bertie's habits—

and he was just working around to the nobbling when Bertie chipped in and said:

"You're fired an' all!"

"Too late, you rat-toothed *ladrone!*" snapped Smitty. "I resigned two minutes ago."

"Good!" sneered Bertie. "That means I needn't pay you nothing! Not even the shilling I'd decided on."

"You——" began Smitty.

"Oh, come on!" murmured Tim, taking his arm. "We're wasting time."

"Yer! *Mine!*" growled Bertie, reaching for the phone. He must have decided by now that the boys had heard nothing. "Blow before I call the Law!"

Smitty would have stayed and argued that point too, but Tim had a good grip and steered him out into the yard.

"If there's anyone calling the Law," he murmured to his squirming pal, "it'll be Louie. When we tell him what I heard."

Chapter 12

LOUIE CALLS IN THE EXPERTS

Louie was not in any hurry to call the police though, as it turned out.

He listened to the boys' story with deep interest. Sitting on his stool behind his desk, he listened carefully to everything they said. He didn't interrupt. His eyes went into slits as the smoke curled slowly up around his ears. But his expression never changed. Even at the juicy bits—even when they told him exactly what Tim had heard—his expression didn't change. The only flicker was from his cigarette lighter, halfway through. The only words he uttered were: "Go on . . . yes . . . go on. . . ."

It was maddening really. They had expected Louie to be as excited as they were. Hopping mad, maybe. Eager to march around to Rely-On-Us Dairies and create a vacancy there for a new "Ass Manager and Head Milman." Stirred, anyway. A bit more hopeful—and showing it.

But when Tim and Smitty had finished, Louie just sat on. His eyes stayed in slits. The smoke still slowly curled. With the slits and the smoke, his face looked a bit like a machine-gun nest, it is true. It did look warlike in a quiet brooding way. But there was no action for a while. Just this brooding silence.

Then Smitty spoke up. *He* was excited if Louie wasn't. He smacked a fist into his other hand and said:

"Well, we got him now!"

There was a movement in the slits. A glint. Very faint, but definitely a glint.

Then Louie shook his head slightly. He blew off a few specks of ash.

"No," he said. "Not really we ain't. Y'see, it's still only your word against theirs. Only *Tim's* really. Two to one. And they'd only think you was making it up. Making an excuse for the stuff found in the bottles. Ner. . . ."

Smitty fell back on making mouth signs. His face didn't *fall* at Louie's words. You couldn't say that. But it started slipping.

"Still," said Louie, rolling his cigarette from the left side of his mouth to the right. "We *have* got something solid to go on now. I'll give you that. Yer. . . . Something definite."

The boys perked up. Louie had asked for "something definite." Those very words. And here he was admitting that they'd *brought* him "something definite." From Louie, this was very high praise. From Louie, this was a rave review. The boys perked up, pleased. They grinned at each other and nodded.

"The hell yer laughing at?" Louie snapped—and this time the glint was quite plain. They could almost see the muzzles of the guns behind those slits.

They stopped grinning. They turned their grins into itching mouths, cheeks. They rubbed and looked away.

"This is no comedy," said Louie, in a quieter voice, brooding again. "It en' even a who-done-it mystery, come to that. It's a how-d'we-*prove*-he-done-it. That's what this is. A problem."

Louie lit a fresh cigarette while they scratched away at their chins and mouths.

"We know Bertie's at the bottom of it," went on Louie. "An' now we know who he got to help him. The thing is to prove it. In court." He leaned forward and put a pile of order books straight. "And to do that—prove it—in court—we need experts."

Smitty sighed, very faintly. If there was any breed of men and women Louie admired it was experts. Especially professional experts. And when Louie got on about experts he'd be at it for hours. He usually started with Adam. "Take the Garden of Eden. Adam. Made a mess of it. Why? Because he wasn't an expert. Can't blame him—he'd only just been made—only just been put there—no training. But if he *had* been an expert gardener he'd a known what to put down for snakes . . ."

So it would go on. Experts through the Ages. Only Louie's chat about Obstacles Faced by Delivery Men (dogs, overgrown paths, jammed gates, etc.) —only that went on longer than his Chat on Experts.

Smitty took a deep breath and a big risk. He cut in quick.

"But what experts are you thinking about in this case, Louie?"

Louie frowned. His lips went tight around his cigarette butt. But he must have realized himself that this was no time for long chats.

"Law experts," he said. "Detective. Maybe finger-print men. A good lawyer. Professionals."

He gave them a look that said: "None of this kids' stuff, amateur detective stuff *here!*"

"You mean you *are* going to call the Law in, then?" asked Tim.

Louie shook his head.

"Not the local Law, 'f that's what yer mean. No. Not yet. I mean my own *private* experts. My own Law men."

He gave the stags on his sweater a proud pat. "But——"

"Harry Skinner," murmured Louie, all broody again. He was staring at the phone on his desk as if it were a fortune teller's crystal ball. "Little scruffy-lookin' kid. Pale. Thin. Allus a sticky nose. Game though." Here Louie's cigarette flipped up with approval. "Very game. Turn out in all weathers, that kid would. Never give in . . . route did him good. Started him filling out. Stopped his nose running. Give him an interest in life. Something to be proud of. Used to be on with Norbert Rigg. Good pair, them. Kept on filling out, growing, after he'd left. Shot up to five-ten in no time. Went for a copper."

"Why—what had the copper done to *him?*" asked Smitty, round-eyed.

"Went to *be* a copper, yer mug! Shaddap while I'm talking . . . Went for a copper, I said. Did well there an' all. Knew he would. Game. Never give up."

Louie leaned back again and looked up at them. His eyes flashed proudly.

"Detective-sergeant Skinner now. Up in Lancashire."

Tim stared at him.

"You mean——? But will he come? *Can* he?"

"*Will* he? A course! *Can* he? Yes. Had a word with him already. Standing by. Ready to take part of his leave. Two days' notice. He'll come all right."

"And the lawyer? You said something about a lawyer."

Louie permitted his cigarette to give a faint grin. Then he leaned forward again, brooding over the phone.

"When I first hired Tubby Hooley," he said, "I

thought I'd made a big mistake. Must have done, I thought. Coulder kicked meself . . . Another little 'un. But fat. Well fed. And very clumsy. Dropped five bottles first morning."

Smitty gasped. Tim winced. This was the first they'd ever heard of Tubby Hooley. But knowing dropped bottles and knowing Louie they felt for that boy like brothers. But there was worse to come.

"Second morning he got three crates tangled up so tight they was a write-off."

Tim and Smitty went pale, backed a pace.

"Third morning . . . third morning he held the route up hour 'n' half. Got his hand stuck in a

bottle. Tryner get a milk note out. Had to call the fire department in the finish . . ."

Louie took a deep breath.

"I made up my mind. Fire him at the end the week. No messing. But then comes Friday. Friday night. Collecting night."

Tim and Smitty shuddered. They crossed their fingers for this boy they'd never seen—never heard of before. They prayed he wouldn't make a mess of *that* job.

"Money was tight at that time," Louie was saying. "Getting some of the customers to put their hands in their pockets was bad enough. Getting 'em to pull 'em out an' pay up was nearly as bad as getting Tubby's hand out that bottle. Bad debts all over town . . ."

Louie took his cigarette out here and daintily flicked ash onto the floor—a rare tribute.

"But on that one Friday," he continued, "Tubby cleared up nearly twenty bad debts. Some of 'em been owing months. All by talking. Arguin'. What he said to 'em nobody ever really got to know. Kid with him said it come out so fast it made him dizzy . . . Anyway, they paid up." Louie sighed and shook his head. "Kept him on—naturally," he added.

"And now he's a lawyer?"

"Now he's a lawyer." Louie plunged a hand up under his sweater and brought out a cigarette pack. Then, from the pack, he drew out a slip of paper. "Arnold G. Hooley," he said, reading. "Arnold G.

Hooley of Smith, Smith, Bagg and Hooley. London. Big route or practice or what they call it. And *he's* ready to come an' all. Called him only yesterday."

Louie flicked ash at the phone.

"Took him about five hundred words to say, 'Yes. Course. Anything for *you*, Lou. Just give us a blow when yer ready for me' . . . But that's what it amounted to."

"And are you—when are you sending for him?"

"Now. Today. For 'em both, 'smarrer fact. And—*here, don't go jumpin' up and down like that!*—listen. You two had better stand by an' all. Might be some work for you."

"Eh?" gasped Smitty. "On the route? Is it picking up, then?"

Louie shook his head.

"No. Not till this lot gets sorted out will that pick up . . . No, not on the route. On the *beat*. With Harry. When I rang him he said he might want some assistants. Copper's runners. He'll brief yer when he gets here."

Chapter 13

TIGER SKINNER

Business must have been slack just then with the criminals of Chorburn in Lancashire.

Maybe they'd all gone on a holiday at the same time. People do that, up there. All the mills and most of the shops shut up for a week or two. Maybe that had happened with the criminals. All the burglars lying on Blackpool sands, working out plans for the coming season. All the car bandits bashing around on the dodge-'ems.

Anyway, Detective-sergeant Skinner didn't need the full two days' notice Louie had mentioned. He was there the next day. He was there waiting for Louie in the shack when Louie got back from the route. He was sitting on the edge of Louie's desk, smoking and staring at Louie's wall maps and lists as if they'd been the faces of wanted men.

That is to say he was staring at them fiercely.

Tim and Smitty had also arrived at the shack early, eager to know if Louie had any news about the next step. They hadn't arrived as early as Detective-sergeant Skinner, though. When they got to the dairy they found the shack with the door open and this man sitting on the edge of Louie's desk, staring at the wall.

And the look of him was so fierce that they hadn't dared go any farther. They hung about the yard instead, and waited for Louie there. They had an idea it might be Skinner, but they weren't taking any chances. It could just as easily have been an angry customer. Someone who was aiming to knock Louie's teeth out.

For Detective-sergeant Skinner hadn't had a shave that morning, which made him look as if he'd been working nights. And his eyes had a raw red-rimmed look. And he held his head hunched down, which made him look hardly tall enough for a detective. And, as already stated, there was this fierce scowl on his face as he dragged away at his cigarette and stared at the map and the lists.

The boys didn't realize it then, but this was how Detective-sergeant Skinner usually looked. A bit scruffy. A bit ruffled. All hunched up as if ready to spring. And very fierce. That was why he was known as "Tiger" Skinner up in Chorburn. From the stubble on his chin and the scruffy look, you might have thought it had been Bertie's route he'd started life on. From the cigarette that was always burning away in the corner of his mouth and that fierce brooding look, you'd have realized it was Louie he'd started with, after all.

Bunched up, coiled up, ready to spring—that was Tiger Skinner. The scruffiness didn't matter much, for Tiger was mainly a night detective. He liked being on nights. He liked nothing better than to throw down his hand of cards and go dashing off to answer an emergency call. He loved chasing about over rooftops in the dark. He gloried in a scrap. Some of the Chorburn criminals used to say the police daren't let him out during the day. They used to say that Tiger was kept in a cell during the day and fed on raw liver. But they were biased.

When Louie arrived, Tim and Smitty followed. The meeting of such a pair of men wasn't to be missed. The boys expected something special from the first meeting of these two—whether the stranger was Detective-sergeant Skinner or only an angry customer.

What they got was this:

"Harry . . ."

"Lou . . ."

"Yer got here, then?"

"Looks like it . . ."

No handshake. No roar of welcome or rage. Just

two cigarettes wagging and two pairs of fierce eyes slowly swiveling up and down.

"Who're these?"

Smitty stepped briskly back onto Tim's toes.

"They're all right. Told 'em you might be able to use 'em."

"Ar . . ."

Slow nods at Tim and Smitty. Thoughtful. Still pretty fierce.

"Course," said Tiger Skinner, turning back to Louie. "Me helping you's not strictly professional etiquette."

"Eh? Professional what?"

"Etiquette."

"You always was one for the big word. Nearly as bad as Tubby Hooley. Like 'tuberculin-tested' for 'redcap.' Now this. Professional eti—— Say it again. Slow."

"Eti- O.K.?"

"Eti- yer, go on."

"-quette—right?"

"Eti-quette—yer. What's it mean? Professional eti-quette?"

"Me coming here helping you. In another force's area. That's *not* professional etiquette. They won't like it."

"They can flaming well lump it, then! What I want's enough evidence to go to the local force *with*. I thought I told you this on the phone."

"Yes. Only I'm just saying. Don't go blabbing about it all over town."

Given to Louie, such a warning would have been an insult. But the detective was looking at Tim and Smitty.

Dry-mouthed, they nodded. They understood.

"Right!" said Skinner. "Now a course——" Being back with Louie again was making him *speak* like Louie. "A course, if this was Chorburn the job would be easy. I'd simply go around to this Bertie Winks and have a few words with him." He made clutching movements with his hands. Tim wondered what sort of words they'd be. Then Tiger Skinner blew the ash off his cigarette—again just like Louie. "Only a course that's not possible here."

"No," said Louie, giving his ex-assistant a faintly worried sideways look. "I was thinking more on the lines of——"

"Yer, yer! I know. Ordinary routine stuff." For a moment Skinner looked rather wistful. Then he leaped off the edge of the desk, nearly making Smitty faint. But it was only to rub his backside. "Anyway, this is getting us nowhere," he said briskly. "You say you kept some of this stuff found in the milk?"

"In the safe," said Louie, nodding grimly toward the main office building. "Wait here."

Left alone with the detective the boys felt about as easy as they would in a cage with a real tiger.

For a minute or so there was another brooding si-

119

lence. The detective glowered at the wall map. Then, with a suddenness that made Tim jump, he grinned and said:

"Does he still get mad if you smash an empty?"

They nodded, feeling a bit easier.

"And if you get an order mixed up?"

From that moment on, the three were firm friends. Not until Louie returned did they fall silent again. He was carrying a tray.

"Lot er laughing goin' on in here," he muttered suspiciously, looking from one to another. "Sounds like a tea party or something."

But Harry Skinner had abandoned his boyhood memories. Tiger Skinner pounced on the tray.

"Let's look," he said, putting it on the desk. "There might be something . . ."

Without touching any of them, he looked hard and carefully at the objects on the tray. These were:

the dried-out milk note;
the dried-out cigarette butt;
the dried-out shoestring;
the dried-out half cuff link; and
the dried-out piece of glass.

"You've not *washed* them, have you?" grunted Skinner.

He sniffed at them.

"Just dried 'em," said Louie. "Can't yer tell?"

"Got a bit of a cold," said Skinner. "Anyway, I'm

glad you haven't washed 'em. You never know." He straightened up and lit a fresh cigarette. "What about the bottle with the fish in it? That sounded the best lead to me."

"Did to me an' all," said Louie, bending down. "Thought I'd better look after this one meself."

He drew a long round biscuit can from the leg of one of his spare rubber boots. He put it on the table.

"Stand back," he said, taking the lid off the can.

They stood back as, gently, Louie tilted it and slid out the bottle onto a sheet of blotting paper.

The milk had been emptied out, but Louie hadn't risked rinsing the bottle. Hence the green mold all over the inside surface. Hence the order to stand back. Hence the extra puffing of cigarettes and the holding of noses. With that bottle on the table, Louie's office suddenly began to look (and smell) more like Bertie Winks's. The tin-foil cap, still slightly crumpled, as it was when Mrs. Bellamy had rescued it from the strainer, fell out onto the blotting paper beside it.

"Should be some fingerprints the outside the bottle," said Louie.

Skinner nodded.

"We'll see," he said. "I'll send it off to our place straightaway. Have it checked. I've made it right with the fingerprint bloke. Pal of mine. He'll be ready for it . . ." Then he frowned. "But what about the fish? That might give us a lead. If it's a rare one."

"Looked like an ordinary goldfish to me," said Louie. "Nothing rare about it. Anyway, I've kept it in the refrigerator at home."

Skinner nodded.

"Good. I'll have a look after. Meanwhile," he said, glancing at Tim and Smitty, "it's no use having the prints on the bottle tested if we've nothing to check them against. And this is where you come in. I want you to get me a set—right hand, left hand, palms, as many as you can get anyway—of that kid's. The one Louie was telling me about over the phone. The one you think did the actual planting."

Chapter 14

ON THE TRAIL WITH THE EXPERT

As Louie never got tired of saying afterward, it was a treat to see an expert at work. A real expert. An expert of the class of Harry Skinner. It was such a treat that Louie almost forgot his troubles as he watched his ex-assistant get down to the job of finding what he could from that trayful of articles.

For though he may have been at his best on night work, Tiger Skinner was no slouch on days. Scrapping with burglars, chasing them over rooftops, searching suspects for hidden guns—these may have been the jobs he liked best. But that didn't mean to say he was too bored to bother with routine stuff. Tigers—he seemed to be reminding Louie and the boys—tigers like hunting, which means stalking as well as springing. Tigers—he seemed also to be reminding them—tigers are members of the cat family. And there is nothing as patient as a cat out hunting, on the trail.

So, in the next few days, Tiger Skinner seemed never to rest. In and out of the dairy, checking with Louie; around and around the town, checking with customers, shopkeepers, or Tim and Smitty—you could never be sure where you'd see him next. You could never be certain that when you turned the next corner you wouldn't be bumping into him—scribbling something in a notebook, or staring with his red-rimmed eyes and thoughtful ferocity at a shop across the street.

There was nothing spectacular at first. Nothing was solved absolutely. Nothing was finally proved. Nothing like a spring was made. It was all stalking. But it was a stalking that got him nearer and nearer the quarry, you could tell.

The shoestring, for instance. All the rumors suggested that this had something to do with Louie's shoe-repairing side line. It was suggested that if Louie hadn't used to deliver and collect shoe repairs for his brother-in-law, this string wouldn't have found its way into a bottle of milk.

"All right, then," Tiger Skinner had said to Louie. "We'll start there. Where's this brother-in-law of yours live?"

And, on the first morning, he had got valuable information from the shoe repairer.

"Definitely not from a pair done by me," he had said.

"How so sure?" Tiger had asked.

"The tag there—see those letters stamped on it?"

"Yes. M.P.R. I was going to ask you . . ."

"Mario Pirelli, Roma . . . Came from a pair of Italian shoes, that lace did. Fairly new ones an' all— still with the makers' laces in 'em. Well-known firm in the trade. Pretty expensive. Never had a pair of them to repair all the time I been here."

So that was something, anyway. Proof that the string had had nothing to do with Louie's repairs.

"Who sells 'em here?" was Tiger's next question.

"No one I know of," said the cobbler. "Been bought in London probably. Or in Italy itself."

"Thanks," said Tiger.

That was something he could follow up later.

The cigarette butt gave him similar information. Negative but useful.

Again the rumors suggested it was one of Louie's, but even Louie himself had killed that one.

"Not my brand," he'd said. "Too expensive. Too mild. Besides, yer never catch me chucking 'em away that long."

"So I notice," Tiger had said, glancing at the floor of the shack. "But there's something else . . ."

Very gently, with the tip of the fine blade of his penknife, he scraped at the dried milk on the butt end.

"See?" he said, blowing. "You don't use lipstick either, do you? Not unless you've changed a lot since I was on the route . . . That was a woman's cigarette."

"You mean it was a *bird* been doing the nobbling as well as the kid?" asked Louie.

His eyes were open pretty wide for him.

"Not necessarily," said Tiger. "Probably a cigarette butt picked up in the street. Where was it found?"

Louie told him.

Tiger nodded.

"I know the place. Near a row of shops. That seems to fit."

"Eh?"

"Fairly expensive brand. Lot of it wasted. Not many women smoke in the street. Those who do don't usually smoke posh brands. And if they *did* they wouldn't chuck 'em away this length. So— this woman comes shopping. In car. Stops at shops. Steps out. Chucks cigarette down. Steps on it . . . And there it was, ready waiting for the kid."

Another negative but useful clue was teased by Tiger from the piece of broken glass.

"See this?" he said, tracing out a raised-up inscription with the tip of his knife.

Again Louie had been doing some thinking of his own.

"Yer," he said. "Letter. Part of a word. J."

126

"Well, then," said Skinner, "it couldn't have been a New Day bottle, could it?"

"No," said Louie. "I know. But whose could it have been?"

"Got a milk-trade directory?"

"Over in the offices."

"Fetch it, then."

But no, not a single dairy operating within a radius of fifty miles could they find that had a J in its name.

Then Tiger had another look at the bit of glass and swore.

"A course!" he growled. "J my foot! It's part of a U. Rely-On-Us!"

Louie gave his bluebirds a fond brisk rub at that.

"Sounds more like!" he murmured, his cigarette end making happy little loops.

The half cuff link was more of a plodding job. Tiger soon established that it was a cheap popular make. It had been selling in dozens at several shops —and that seemed to be that, as far as Louie and the boys could see.

Not Tiger, though. There was the question of how *long* they'd been on the market—and the answer to that was two years. Then there was the question of how long they were likely to last without breaking—and the answer to that varied from three to thirty years, according to the shop. Given reasonable wear, they all added.

"All right, then," Tiger would next ask. "So you won't have had many complaints, then? And those you have had you'll have remembered?"

So far, this line of inquiry hadn't brought anything definite. But he was working on it, Tiger was. Shop by shop, clerk by clerk, all down the list.

He was working, too, on the goldfish. Having made a careful note of its size and color and all its markings, he was inquiring at the pet shops and tropical fish clubs—so far without success. For it *was* a goldfish and they were so common.

"Still, it'll come in as a clincher," he said, when he told Louie about it afterward.

"Clincher?"

"Something that'll clinch the case. Top it off. When we do pin-point it to somebody—this Kelly kid probably—when one of the other leads points to him for sure. Then the fish'll come in as a clincher. We'll be able then to ask his parents, relatives—any dead goldfish in the family. Any *missing* goldfish. We can't ask 'em that now. Not till we get something more definite. But then—yes."

Like Louie and the boys, Skinner felt pretty sure that the Kelly boy had been the one who'd actually done the fixing. And what the detective was counting on most was the result of the fingerprint check. At first, however, he'd had great hopes about the milk note too.

"If this is his handwriting," he had said, "we've got him even if the prints let us down."

But a good detective always tries to *dis*prove his theories as well as *prove* them. He checks both ways. And Tiger was a very good detective.

"Recognize the writing?" he first asked Louie.

The scrap of cardboard had had a good soaking, of course. The original note was in pencil and faint.

"Can't say for sure," Louie had had to admit.

"Any specimens? Genuine milk notes?"

Louie had a few. But these were difficult ones that he used as examples to show people how tough his job was, or to test new boys with. None of them matched the note that had been found in the milk. Nor did the writing on any of the customers' letters that Tiger got him to hunt up in the office files.

"Suppose we can't go round *every* customer and ex-customer asking for samples," Louie had murmured, giving Tiger a sideways look.

"What makes you suppose that?" grunted Tiger, lighting a fresh cigarette. "We can if we're stuck. And we will." Then he gave the note a thoughtful red-rimmed stare. "Only I think we can save ourselves the bother. It's just occurred to me . . ."

He reached out for Louie's pile of notebooks.

"Still use the red for complaints?"

Louie nodded. Skinner flipped it open.

"This was found in the bottle on—when? What date? Where?"

"Here," said Louie, taking the book from him and flipping the pages himself. "There. That one."

Skinner nodded. Stared hard. Sighed.

"Thought so," he said. "I was afraid that 'ud be it."

"You lookin' at the right page?" Louie asked—for Skinner's stare had seemed to settle on the opposite one.

"I'm looking at this other complaint," said the detective. "Two doors away. The day after. Asking why you didn't leave the two extra pints they'd ordered."

"Ah . . ."

Tim and Smitty had been listening to this lot. Tim had suddenly seen what Skinner was getting at.

"Yes—ah," said the detective. "The nobbler simply nicked that note before Louie got there and shoved it in next-door-but-one's milk after he'd gone. This Kelly kid deliver papers both these houses?"

"I—we——"

Smitty looked at Tim and Tim looked at Smitty.

"Well, check then," said Skinner. "While you're on with the fingerprints."

"Yer!" said Louie. He was feeling a bit sore at having been so near to the culprit without noticing anything. Why, the paper boy must have been only a few yards away, hiding, waiting for Louie to deliver at that house! "And when you gonner come up with something, eh?" he snapped at Tim and Smitty.

"You been two days now, after his fingerprints, and you haven't come up with a thing."

"It—it's not so easy," said Tim. "We——"

"Amateurs!" growled Louie.

"Not at all," said Tiger Skinner. "It isn't easy for anyone, that job, I'll tell you! But keep trying, lads. It's probably the most important of the lot."

The look on Louie's face just then ought to have been painted in oils and hung up on the wall. With this title: *Contradicted! In His Own Shack! In Front of His Assistants! By an Ex-Assistant! On a Subject High on the List of his Favorite Chats: Dabblers versus Experts.*

But there was nothing he could say this time. Just nothing. And he knew it.

After all, Tiger was the expert and you don't argue with experts.

Giving the detective a grateful look and trying not to look *too* triumphant, the boys left the shack—more determined than ever to get those prints.

Chapter 15

ON THE TRAIL
WITH THE AMATEURS

Tiger Skinner was right. Getting fingerprints without letting their owner know is never an easy job. If you live with the person it isn't too bad. If you work with him it isn't too bad. If you go to school with him it isn't too bad. If you're a friend of his it isn't too bad.

But if you don't know him very well—and if he doesn't like you, anyway—and if he's a bit suspicious of you—and if you haven't a hope of getting into his house or his school or his place of work—it's tough. Even Tiger Skinner would have found it tough. Hadn't he admitted as much?

Luckily, all this happened in the school holidays. Tim and Smitty had all day every day in which to do the job. If they hadn't, it might have taken them till Christmas. As it was, well— . . .

On the first day they hadn't the faintest idea how hard it would be. In fact, Smitty himself thought it would be the opposite.

"Dead easy!" he said. "Look. I've brought this from home. Found it in a drawer. Used to be my dad's before he give up smoking."

He was holding a cigarette case. It was a chromium one. It was a bit scratched, a bit dented here and there, but it was still mainly smooth and shiny. He was holding it up, his thumb under the bottom edge and a finger over the top edge.

"He used to use it as a shaving mirror in the Army—*no! don't touch!*" Smitty pulled his arm back as Tim reached out. "Want to keep it nice and clear. So his prints'll stand out."

"Your dad's?"

"No, *imbecile!* Kelly's! Come on, he'll be just finishing his paper route. We'll catch him outside his house on his way home."

It was a very cunning plan. Only someone with an Italian mother could have worked it out. But . . .

"Hey! Have you dropped this?" called Smitty, outside Kelly's house.

Kelly turned, frowning a bit when he saw who it was.

Smitty approached him, holding the case the way he'd held it for Tim.

Kelly's eyes opened a bit wider.

"'S have a look," he said.

Nudging Tim, Smitty gave it to Kelly. Then they watched as Kelly turned it over in his hands. Their hearts rejoiced at the thought of all those lovely prints going onto it. But those same rejoicing hearts missed a beat, three or four seconds later.

"Yes!" said Kelly, breaking into a grin. "Yes, it is mine. Dropped it on my way out. Won it at a fair. It's not worth much so I can't give you a reward, but thanks all the same. Ta!"

And with that, he slipped it into his pocket and went for his breakfast.

That's when they realized it wasn't going to be easy.

But it was a hot morning and Smitty had another idea.

When Kelly left his house again he found them sitting on a garden wall at the end of the street. They were swinging their legs and drinking orange juice out of bottles.

"Still waiting for a reward?" he asked, grinning in that nasty way of his.

Smitty shrugged.

"Reward? What reward?" He pretended he didn't know what Kelly was talking about. "Want a drink?" he asked, handing out his half-emptied bottle.

Kelly sniffed.

"Not when you've been at it," he said. "Don't want foot-and-mouth disease."

135

"That's all right," said Smitty, reaching down behind the wall. He'd got another three fulls stashed away down there, besides two empties they'd drunk while waiting. "Here's a new 'un."

Kelly looked at it without reaching for it. His face looked very suspicious. "Oh, what a nasty suspicious mind he's got!" thought Tim—or words to that effect.

Then Kelly shook his head.

"Ner!" he sneered. "I know what you've done. You've put some working mixture in it, haven't you? Some laxative or something. You've doctored it up. Just to get your own back because I wouldn't give you a reward . . . Well, hard lines!"

And again he walked away.

"I wouldn't mind," said Smitty, watching him go, "I wouldn't mind if he'd been suspicious about the right thing! But this is wicked. *Scelleratissimo!*"

"Never mind," said Tim. "Let's get after him. See what he touches."

What they saw Kelly touch, on that day and the day after included:

one bus;
his bike;
three pedestrian handrails;
his garden gate (several times);
his house door (also several times);
one cigarette machine (they nearly cried, he left
    such lovely prints on that);

one shop window (they could have kicked it in
    and run off with the bit with his prints on);
one car;
one lamppost;
six or seven shop-door handles;
about as many shop counters;
one park bench; and
the back of a truck.

It was maddening. How could they wrap up a lamppost or a bus and send *that* to Tiger's fingerprint man? Or any of the other things for that matter? Only once did they have a chance with something suitable. This was when he went into a snack bar.

"Aha!" sang Smitty, as they watched him go inside. "We might be on to something here!"

They watched through the window as Kelly gave his order. They watched as he took his milk shake to a table. They almost drooled as they saw him suck it dry—not because they were thirsty but because of all the lovely prints going onto the glass.

"Come on!" said Smitty, the moment Kelly left. "That's ours!"

"But—we can't just *steal* it!" gasped Tim, following him.

"You watch me!" said Smitty. "Just you order a couple of lemonades and watch."

Tim ordered the lemonades and watched. He watched Smitty go up to the table Kelly had left.

He watched his pal pull out a chair, roughly. He watched the table shake, with the roughness. He watched Kelly's glass roll over onto the floor with the shaking. He saw it break.

Crash!—sh!—sh!—sh!

In one large piece and several smaller ones.

"I'm sorry!" cried Smitty. "I'm very sorry! How much I owe you?"

"Three shillings," said the woman behind the counter. "Herbert!"

"Here you are, then," said Smitty, handing the money over. Then he turned to the bits. "Hey, *no!*"

Already the man called Herbert was sweeping them up. He paused. A pleasant man. Smiling.

"What?" he said.

"Leave 'em!" said Smitty. "We want *them.*"

"Ha! ha!" laughed the man, going on sweeping.

"No! Honest!" cried Smitty. "They're ours, them bits! I just paid for 'em. Didn't I?"

"Ha! ha!" laughed the man. "Real joker, you are!"

"Heh! heh!" laughed his wife. "Breaks the morning up nicely, a joke does!"

Smitty looked as if he could have broken her up nicely.

"No—I mean it—I—here—let me—save your legs . . ."

He tried to take the shovel and its bits off Herbert.

But the man had a broad back and it was turned and Smitty couldn't get around it.

"I'll give you *another* three shillings for the bits!" poor Smitty nearly screamed. "I promise you!"

"Har! har! har!"

Herbert's back shook as he went through the door into the kitchen.

"Har! har! har!" they heard him roar, as he slid the precious bits into a bin or something.

"You'll be the death of him!" moaned the woman. "Making him laugh like that! Oh dear, *me* too! Here, have another lemon. On the house."

That was some consolation, anyway—but not much.

"If only he'd touch something small, somewhere *outside!*" groaned Smitty afterward.

"Yes," said Tim, bringing back some of his lemonade with disgust. "If——"

Then he stopped.

"Mugs!" he said.

"Eh?" said Smitty. "En't you had enough with glassware?"

"Us, I mean!" cried Tim. "For not thinking. He touches dozens of small things. Every morning. On his paper route."

"What you mean?"

"His papers. The papers themselves. The papers he delivers. Listen . . ."

Next morning, armed with about half a dozen folded newspapers of their own, Tim and Smitty

followed in Kelly's wake. Their own folded papers were to keep them on the right side of the Law. They took them along to replace the ones they hoped to snitch from the letter boxes. The ones with Kelly's prints on them.

But alas! There are newspaper boys and newspaper boys. In four main categories:

1. There are newspaper boys who are *idle* and stick the papers in the garden gates.

2. There are newspaper boys who are *athletic* and throw the papers like darts, into the front porches.

3. There are newspaper boys who are *ordinary mild* newspaper boys who simply stick the papers in the letter-box slots in the house doors and pass on. And:

4. There are newspaper boys who are *cheeky*. These are boys who have been told off for using Methods 1 and 2—even threatened with the sack. So they do the exact opposite. They'll pop a paper through the slot, like loading a gun, then BAM —they give the end of the paper such a bash it shoots right up the hall. Then they go off sniggering.

Kelly was one of these.

Tim and Smitty might have known it.

In the whole of the route there was only one house where he hadn't tried to shoot the paper up the hall and through the kitchen door. A house where they took *The Times*.

No doubt he'd been told off there for Method 4 as well as 1 and 2.

So what he'd done was stick it in the letter box exactly half and half. No more. No less. He'd stuck *The Times* in that letter box so exactly it could nearly have been called cheeky in itself. And, just to drive his point home, he'd taken care to scratch the paper slightly, just where the spring flap touched it. This was so that when they pulled it from inside, a strip would be torn off and they'd only have themselves to blame.

But Tim and Smitty weren't interested in the tricks of paper boys. They weren't interested in Kelly's feud with the people who took *The Times*. All they were worried about was the chance of getting his fingerprints, and when they saw that paper sticking out they could have cheered.

"Quick!" said Smitty. "Let's get it while it's there!"

But alas again!

The Times reader had had the same idea at the same time. When Smitty grasped the half outside, the reader was just grasping the half inside. When Smitty tugged, the reader tugged.

At first Smitty thought it was the letter-box flap that was extra-strong, so he tugged harder. At first the reader thought it was Kelly up to his tricks again and *he* tugged harder. It was a bit like pulling a party favor cracker.

But *The Times* is a tough thick paper and can stand a lot of tugging. And the only explosion came from the reader.

"Let go, damn you!" the reader roared.

And Smitty for the moment thought the letter box itself had spoken. He let go from sheer fright, rapidly crossing himself.

"I'll have the police on you for this!" roared the reader, crashing away at the bolts. By now he'd got around to suspecting newspaper bandits at work rather than another nasty Kelly trick. "I'll teach you to try to steal my *Times!*"

But also by now Tim and Smitty had reached the

corner of the street, and were leaving the district fast.

There's nothing like a bit of encouragement, though.

After all these failures, they were beginning to think they'd never get Kelly's fingerprints. They were beginning to think of themselves as a real pair of bungling amateurs. Then Tiger Skinner said his few kind words in front of Louie and the whole picture changed. It was as if the best idea had been frozen up in Tim's mind all the time. It was as if all that had been needed to thaw it out were Detective-sergeant Skinner's kind words.

"Course!" Tim cried, before they'd even got out of the dairy yard. "Why didn't we think of it before? It never fails!"

The next morning, the boy Kelly paused in his delivering. It was at a house with a nice big garden, lots of bushes, and a porch. He was just about to bash the folded paper clean through the box and halfway up the stairs, when something caught his eye.

A small metal box, gleaming with glossy red paint. A biscuit box that someone had been smartening up. On the floor of the porch. With a notice next to it—a piece of cardboard with the scrawled words:

WET PAINT
PLEASE DO NOT
TOUCH

143

"Go on!" muttered Kelly, bending down. "Bet it's dried."

The words DO NOT meant nothing to him. PLEASE left him cold.

"Hasn't though!" he murmured, straightening up with two red fingertips. Then, after scraping his fingers dry on the brick wall and bashing the paper through the letter box, he left without giving the matter another thought.

When he had gone, two figures stepped out of the bushes at the side of the garden path.

"Success!" hissed one.

"A pair of beauties!" hissed the other, carefully picking up the sticky box by its corners. "Perfect!"

144

Chapter 16

ARNOLD G. HOOLEY

It's hard to tell how the boys would have lasted out during the next twenty-four hours or so. It's hard to tell how they could have kept themselves from breaking up into little pieces with impatience. It's hard to tell how they'd have stuck it if it hadn't been for Arnold G. Hooley.

Tiger Skinner sent off the box as soon as they brought it to him. He packed it carefully, lovingly, and mailed it express to his pal.

Opinion please by phone. Urgent.
Call us here 3 p.m. tomorrow (23rd).

That was the note he sent with it.

"Three o'clock?" grunted Louie. "Why so late? Why not mornin'?"

145

"Give him time to check 'em properly," said Tiger. "And in case he's busy on something else."

It was hard to take, but it made sense. So three o'clock it was.

This left a bit over twenty-four hours to wait. Twenty-nine to be exact. And twenty-nine hours can be a long time if you're waiting for information of that sort. Information on which your whole future might depend.

Luckily, Arnold G. Hooley arrived that very morning. He rolled up in a large rented car about an hour after they'd posted off the red box. He stepped out of the car and into Louie's shack like visiting royalty. All he needed was a party of local councilors fussing around him.

Tubby, yes. He was still tubby, but tall with it, so it wasn't just that. It was something about him—something smooth and tight and firm and polished . . . Yes. Probably that was it. That polished look. Smooth without being oily. Glossy without being greasy.

His head was bald but brown and polished. He looked nearly as old as Louie, but of course he couldn't have been. His face had that same smooth-shaven look that Louie's had, but browner and plumper. What bit of hair he had, around his ears and at the back, was rich and brown. It was so well polished it looked like part of his skin—a different colored part of his skin. And that again reminded you of Louie in a way.

146

And, just like Tiger Skinner, he seemed to have caught Louie's cigarette-wagging trick. His mouth was rarely without a cigarette, so that it wagged when he spoke. Only his cigarettes were stuck in a long, shiny syrup-colored holder, which made them wag in wider, more graceful arcs.

That was the end of any likeness, though. For where both Louie and Tiger seemed to have chucked on any old clothes, Arnold G. Hooley was a dresser. Tim and Smitty had never seen such a splendid suit, brown and faintly shiny. They hadn't known collars could be got so white as the one that cut into Hooley's plump brown neck. They liked his shirt, too, with its broad pink stripes, and Smitty would have gone without dinners for a month for a pair of brown suède shoes as smart as Hooley's. He smelled good too—sharp and spicy.

But it wasn't his looks or his smell that had them spellbound. It was the way he spoke. They had never—Tim and Smitty—in all their lives heard anything like this. Let's study a sample—the words Hooley spoke on meeting Louie that morning. There's no need to try to puzzle them out. A rough translation will be given at the end. Just look at them. Just sit back and enjoy the look of them and try to imagine what they sounded like to Louie, Tiger, and the boys.

"Ah, Lewis, how extraordinarily nice to renew our acquaintanceship, albeit in such somewhat depressing circumstances! How absolutely extraordinarily pleasing! And goodness me—I must say you don't appear to have undergone any radical transformation whatsoever, no, not a single hair do you appear to have shed, not a gray thread to be seen, everything so absolutely delightfully and so—I was almost on the point of saying so *disconcertingly*, though, of course, that isn't the *mot juste* in this particular case, far from it—so *strangely*, shall we say, so *peculiarly* the same!"

Which meant: "Hi, Lou! Nice to see you. You haven't changed a bit."

Another sample went like this (again there's no need to puzzle it out, the answer's at the end):

"Naturally, I was more than disconcerted, I was

positively distressed to hear of your present—ah—predicament—your present—ah—perhaps contretemps would be a better word, for, of course, I'm perfectly sanguine about the outcome—always given that minimum element of good fortune without which even the most watertight of cases might well find itself in somewhat tricky navigational straits. As I say, I was distressed to get your message, but absolutely, positively, unquestionably delighted to feel that I could be of some small assistance."

Which meant: "Sorry about the mess you're in, but don't worry. We'll see what we can do."

As Louie said to the others, on the quiet:

"He gets his words into a bigger tangle 'n he used to get them crates."

To which Tiger Skinner, who'd met quite a number of lawyers in his career replied:

"Yes. But *he* knows what he's talking about. And it's not so much the way these fellers talk that counts. Not at this stage, anyway. It's the way they *listen*."

Be that as it may, we shall in future quote only what Arnold's words amounted to. What he actually *said* will from time to time be put in footnotes, and those who like doing word puzzles can get on with it there.

"And I must say," Tiger Skinner added to the last remark, "I like the way he acts. I like the way he gets cracking, gets organized."

This, too, was a good point. For within a couple

of hours of his arrival, Hooley had organized himself a large office in the dairy's main building. And
not only had he organized this large office, he had
also taken over:

a spare filing cabinet;
the biggest desk in the place;
two telephones;
a bottle of the directors' sherry;
an electric typewriter;
stacks of paper;
three bottles of different colored inks;
a dictaphone;
the firm's cat (it never stopped purring from the
    moment it set eyes on him); and
Mr. Peters's favorite shorthand typist.

"It will be better for working in," he explained
about the office. "It will give us more elbow room."[1]
And indeed he was right. What with all the com-
ings and goings of Tiger and the boys, Louie's
shack had started to get a bit untidy. Now, in the
office that Hooley had taken over, everything had
its place and nothing was in danger of getting
overlooked.

The articles that had been planted in the milk all

[1] What he actually said was: "I'm rather inclined to the opinion
that our task will be expedited were we to offer ourselves the
advantages of a larger temporary headquarters than is provided
by your own comfortable but nonetheless somewhat confined
accommodation, Lewis."

had special drawers in the filing cabinet. With each article was a bunch of notes that Tiger Skinner had made. With each bunch of Tiger's notes were further notes, made by Louie and the boys, about the place where the article was found, the name of the customer, the time, and so on. Then there was a special file for information about the articles that had *not* been handed in—with notes of all *their* details. Then there were files about the people concerned—Bertie and the Kelly boy in particular, with an extra wodge of notes about Gilbert Dabbit himself. And there was, of course, a file for the summons (which Arnold G. Hooley read *very* closely, *very* slowly, at least three times) with notes about the false-teeth complaint.

Nor was this all. Every batch of notes about every article or complaint or person had been gone over by Hooley. He had gone over every batch and decided which were the most important points. Then he had got the shorthand typist to prepare a *master file* of the main points of the whole case. This was on his desk in a pink folder. All he had to do to refresh his memory was flip through this master file. Thus, inside twenty-four hours, the whole thing was at his fingertips.

But it wasn't simply a question of sorting things out.

All this time, Tiger was coming in with fresh information and this had to be added to the rest. Then again, Hooley seemed to have a thing about looking at it from all angles. With him, it wasn't just a case of finding enough evidence to prove that Bertie and the boy had tampered with the milk. With him, it was also a case of what to do if they *couldn't* find enough evidence. Or what to do if any fresh nobbling took place. And what to do next even if they did find the evidence and prove Bertie's guilt. How best to present their case. At what stage to put the matter into the hands of the local police. And what to do—after everything else had been done, to let the greatest number of customers know the result as soon as possible, and so get their trade back.

All this called for chat after chat: Hooley with Louie; Hooley with Tiger; Hooley with Louie and Tiger; Hooley with Mr. Peters and Tiger; Hooley with Mr. Peters, Louie, and Tiger. And all these chats had to be noted by the shorthand girl, and all the notes typed, and all the main points put in Hooley's pink file.

The boys were bewildered by it all. But they liked to watch Hooley at work. Like the cat on the window sill, Tim almost felt he could have purred at times. Purred with the pleasure of watching all this smooth activity.

Even Louie had to admit he felt much better to have everything pass through those podgy brown hands. They might have had a few milk bottles slip through them in their time, Louie seemed to be thinking. But on a job like this they couldn't have been safer.

It wasn't until that telephone call came through that a little of this confidence slipped away. It wasn't until then that Tim and Smitty began to wonder if, after all, Arnold G. Hooley was as smart as he seemed.

For, hardly had Tiger Skinner had time to put the phone down and say, "That's it! They're Kelly's prints all right!"—than Hooley started raising doubts.

"Yurray!" yelled Smitty, startling the cat off the window sill. *Bene! Bene!*

"Smashing!" agreed Tim, full of pride at having got that specimen set of prints.

"Good enough!" grunted Louie, looking happier than he'd done for weeks.

"We've got 'em now!" growled Tiger Skinner, glaring around with red-rimmed triumph.

All these things were said and done at roughly the same time. All these things and Hooley's slow shake of the head.

Louie was first to see it.

"Eh?" he said, with a wag of his cigarette. "'S marrer?"

"It won't do, I'm afraid,"[1] said Hooley, making his own cigarette at the end of the holder go down in little dips, as on a graph.

[1] This time those were his exact words. He could be crisp in times of stress, could Hooley.

"What do you mean?" asked Skinner—and his cigarette seemed to stab rather than wag.

"I mean this," said Arnold G. Hooley, looking very serious. "We have the boy's prints on one of the tampered-with bottles. Very well. We can now *prove* them to be his. Better still. But——" The word came out like a bullet. "*But,* gentlemen, where does that get us? A little farther, I agree. A good step farther, I'll allow. But not all the way. For consider. Where were the original prints found? On a milk bottle. Whose prints are they? A paper boy's."

There was dead silence in the office now. Hooley broke it by flipping open the pink folder.

"A paper boy who is no fool, by all accounts. One might even say a *cunning* young scamp. Well then, gentlemen . . ." Hooley sat back and spread his fingers out, thumbs nearly touching, butterfly fashion. "All he need say is, *Yes. Of course they're mine. I noticed the bottle was tilted when I was delivering my paper. Leaning against the door in danger of falling. So I straightened it.* Or he could say he'd picked it up to inspect a strange insect he'd seen crawling up the side. Or for any one of a dozen reasons a boy like that could make up. And with his best dark suit on, a few tears, a good lawyer, and a reasonably soft judge he'd be sure to get away with it."

In the dead, shocked, saddened silence, Arnold G. Hooley slowly shook his head.

"I'm sorry. But there it is," he said.

Skinner nodded.

"He's right," he murmured. "You tend to overlook these things when you're on the job."

Louie said nothing for a moment. He was busy taking something out of his mouth and putting it in the wastepaper basket. While Hooley had been speaking he had put a fresh cigarette in his mouth. Tim couldn't be sure whether he'd actually got around to lighting it or not—but he'd certainly come near to swallowing it.

Louie wiped the last of the chewed remains from his mouth and turned around. His eyes were screwed up with fury, amazement, disbelief, despair.

"What—what *can* we do, then?" he growled. "Eh? Tell me. What you're here for. Tell me. Go on. If them prints en' any good, what *is?* Eh? You tell me. *What?*"

"Ah, well now," said Hooley, and his voice was so smooth that even Louie began to look less sore. "I've been thinking about that. I've been giving a lot of careful thought to that. As I say, all this—this evidence—it's fine, admirable. The more we have, the better. But it is only *supporting* evidence. It only serves to back our theory up. It doesn't *prove* anything . . . The thing that could really do the trick is *this* . . . Ah—just close that window, Timothy, would you! . . . Yes. What we really need is *this* . . ."

Chapter 17

WITH GUEST STAR,
NORBERT RIGG

"So that's it, gentlemen. What we need is full proof
of a conversation of this sort."

Arnold G. Hooley's cigarette holder made graceful but firm swoops and loops as he spoke. And on
the words "this sort" he tapped one of the notes
he'd got in his pink folder. His brown plump finger
tapped one of the notes in his pink plump folder.

It was a note about the chat that Tim had heard
when he was on the route with Bertie Winks. The
chat that Bertie had been having with Kelly.

"You mean where they're both talking about what
they did?" said Tiger Skinner. His red-rimmed eyes
now had a gleam in them. His cigarette stabbed the

air in the spaces cut out by Hooley's cigarette's graceful curves. "That it?"

Hooley bent his head in a slow deep nod. The sharp edge of his collar bit deep into his plump neck.

"Exactly," he said. "If we had a record of such a conversation we should have the whole thing tied up. If we had a record of such a conversation—witnessed by adults, of course," he added, with an apologetic smile for Tim. "Well, the case would be complete. We should—as you have put it, Harold —we should have *got* 'em!"

Louie's cigarette wagged. It was getting into a kind of Dance of the Three Cigarettes in the space above the pink folder.

"You mean a tape recording?"

Hooley gave a slight shudder.

"Goodness, no! Not that sort. They're too easy to fake. Very few courts look kindly on records of that kind. No. Just a careful note taken of what is said. By a shorthand writer if possible."

Five pairs of eyes and three cigarettes turned toward the shorthand typist, who'd just come in with the tea. She nearly dropped the lot.

"Miss Jones here could do it admirably," said Hooley, with a smooth brown bow that had her blushing. "But—ah—as I said before—the most important thing is to have several adult witnesses. Independent witnesses. Men of character, of good reputation. Men who will be able to swear to what they heard—and be believed."

Skinner shrugged. He took his cup of tea from the tray, sipped, and pulled a face.

"Yes, but *how?*" he grunted. "We can't go following Bertie's truck around with a troop of witnesses. Just in the hope he'll have another chat with the Kelly kid."

Hooley smirked. He took a small silver tube from his vest pocket, opened it, and tipped out a non-fattening sweetening pill. This he popped into his tea.

"No," he said. He took a sip. "But these things can be *arranged*. For instance, if the man Winks were to have a phone call from the boy Kelly . . . And if the boy Kelly were to say that something urgent had cropped up and he must meet him to talk to him about it . . . And if the boy Kelly, shortly afterward were to have a call from the man Winks . . . And if the man Winks should say something similar . . . And if they both arranged to meet at the same place—during the hours of darkness—a place with plenty of cover for witnesses . . . Well, then!"

Arnold G. Hooley was beaming. He was purring. He was so pleased with himself he popped an extra sweetening pill into his tea.

Louie wasn't anything like so pleased.

"Yer!" he growled. "I can see 'em doing *that!* And—yer!" He waved down the remark the lawyer was about to make. "I know what you're gettin' at.

To *fake* the phone calls. To take their voices off. Imitate them. Easier said ner done."

Hooley still wasn't shaken. Still beaming, still purring, he said:

"Not if an expert impersonator were to do it. A trained actor. A professional mimic. Someone who is a master at 'taking people off,' as you call it."

Skinner grunted. The gleam that had gone from his eyes now came back.

"You mean——"

"Norbert Rigg, the——"

The lawyer was interrupted by a deep sigh from the corner. At the mention of this great movie hero, Miss Jones had nearly swooned. They glared at her. "Shaddap!" snapped Louie—then, remembering she was only a girl, he added: "Miss! . . . Yer, go on," he went on, turning back to Hooley.

"Norbert Rigg. The man Harold here was telling me about over coffee last night. The one who used to be on the route with him. *He'd* be ideal, would he not?"

Louie frowned.

"Yer, but—maybe he wouldn't want. Maybe he's busy. Maybe——"

"'For Louie,'" said Arnold G. Hooley, "and I quote—'For Louie, anything.' Those were his words to me over the phone last night." The lawyer looked at his watch. "In fact he should be here within the next half hour."

There was a crash from the corner. Miss Jones

had fainted. When they'd revived her and sent her off to the rest room, Louie said:

"What about witnesses? These respectable reliable blokes you was on about?"

"I've arranged that too," smiled the lawyer, popping his fourth sweetener into his second cup. "I've arranged for a number of men of—ah—some importance—indeed, I might say *eminence*—to be on hand."

But he wouldn't say who they were. In any case, before they could really get asking him, a white-faced Miss Jones came swaying into the room.

"He's—aw!—he's *here!*" she gasped.

Then fainted again.

Despite Miss Jones's reaction, Norbert Rigg was a bit of a disappointment. In looks, that is.

There was nothing wrong, of course, about the looks of the big cream Mercedes he'd left parked in the dairy yard. But the man himself . . .

Well, he wasn't as tall as you might have expected. He wasn't anything like as tall as Louie, Tiger, or Arnold Hooley, and only a little bit bigger than Tim and Smitty (taken separately, you understand). Then again, there was his face. Very homely, very muddy-looking—rather *pock-marked*, to be quite honest. Skinner said afterward this wasn't unusual with movie stars and actors. It's easy to make them look taller on the screen or stage, he said. And a rough face gave a better surface for the make-up they stuck onto it.

Anyway, Norbert Rigg had arrived, that was the main thing—this little squirt of a man with a dirty yellow sweater, old blue jeans, ankle boots, and cigarette. Yes, cigarette. His mouth, too, never seemed to be without one wagging away there, so that made four of them at it. Only Norbert's was a brown one. "French," whispered Smitty. "Doesn't it stink?"

Norbert didn't say much. After winking at Louie, and digging Skinner in the ribs, and bowing to Hooley, and ruffling the boys' hair, and patting Miss Jones on the shoulder (which sent her straight back to the rest room, weeping and smiling and swearing she'd never have that dress cleaned again, ever) —after these introductions, he listened.

"I see," he said, "I see," when they'd finished telling him all about their plan. "Well, let's swing straight into production, hey?"

And so saying he picked up the phone and asked them to get him Bertie's number at the Rely-On-Us Dairies.

They all stood silent, watching him, as a faint crackling came through. Tim and Smitty, who could picture the scene at the other end, hoped Bertie's receiver wasn't too choked up with flies.

"Ah, Mr. Winks! The *Dairy World and Milkman's Weekly* here!"

They gaped, hardly able to believe that the

fruity elderly voice had come from behind that same wagging brown cigarette.

"We're running a series of articles on the subject of staggered deliveries," continued Norbert, in the same voice. "And I'd like to know what a milkman of your long experience thinks about it . . ."

Where Norbert got his ideas for questions from, none of the others knew. No doubt his boyhood experience on the route with Louie helped. But to hear him chatting with Bertie, you'd have thought he'd been in the milk trade all his life. Everything came so pat, and there was no need to ask him at the end whether Bertie had fallen for it or not. The point was: Had Norbert heard enough of Bertie's voice to be able to imitate him well enough to fool Kelly?

"Hm!" grunted Louie, blowing off with his nose a good inch and a half of ash. "How yer make out, then?"

"Aw, not ser bad, Louie me old sport," came the answer. "I reckon I got the hang of how he . . . talks 'n' that . . . now."

They gasped. At least Louie, Tim, and Smitty gasped. For this was Bertie Winks to the life. Norbert couldn't possibly have *known* what caused it, but he'd even caught, in those little snuffling pauses marked with three dots, the effect of Bertie's nose-picking!

"All right, then . . . eh?" asked Norbert, still in Bertie's voice.

It was more than all right. It was so good Louie looked as if he could have choked him. It was so good you almost *felt* the presence of Dirty Bertie in the room.

Arnold G. Hooley's nose wrinkled.

Tiger Skinner made clutching motions.

The cat got up and walked out.

Then: "All *right?*" cried Louie. "Nobby, that was brilliant!"

Norbert Rigg, winner of three Oscars and holder of two trunks crammed full of admiring press reviews, flushed with pleasure. "Brilliant" was a word that Louie Lay used so rarely he hardly knew how to pronounce it. It was praise indeed.

Then Norbert blinked and, in his normal voice, he said:

"Right, then! Now I'll have a word with this Kelly chappie . . ."

Chapter 18

BERTIE MAKES A DATE

Later that afternoon, Bertie Winks sat back in his shack, put his feet on his junk heap of a desk, and sighed.

He was a very happy man. His nostrils glowed with contentment. Even the popping pale-blue-eyed side of his face looked happy, while the brown-eyed side cracked wide open in a smile. Cracked open like mud in strong sunlight.

For Bertie Winks had had a good day.

True, true—he'd had no assistants to help him on his route. There'd been no rush to replace Tim and Smitty. But that's where being made assistant manager as well as head milkman came in handy. All Bertie had needed to do was lop off chunks of his own route and give them to the other men who worked for Rely-On-Us. Let *them* do the sweating. Why should *he* work his fingers to the bone? With all his paperwork, an' all!

So Bertie had left himself with about six streets and all morning to do them in. And that was one cause of his happiness.

Another cause was two winners at York.

And another cause was the phone call he'd had earlier that afternoon. Some milk trade magazine. Feller asking questions. Nice feller. Seemed to know a bit about the position: how Bertie was one of the best milkmen in the country.

Bertie leaned farther back, stirring a cloud of dust with his feet and disturbing one of his bluebottle friends.

"Wonder who told the feller about how good I am?" murmured Bertie to the fly. "You, yer little blue rastal, eh?"

When Bertie talked like this to the flies he was feeling on top of the world.

"Anyway," murmured Bertie, "it'll do *me* a bit er good. Said he was gonner build the article round me. Send a photographer around for me picture. Bet old Louie'll go green when he hears about it. Which he *will*," added Bertie, giving his nose a firm poke. "I'll tell him meself."

He turned to his pin-ups and gave them a wink that ought to have curled them up at the edges. When Bertie winked like this at his pin-ups he was feeling more than on top of the world. He was feeling so happy he could have taken off for a walk into space.

"I——"

What he was going to say to his pin-ups will never be known. Whatever words of wit or wisdom he was about to utter were blown clean out of his mind. For just then the phone rang again. A startled squadron of bluebottles took off on a low-level flight around Bertie's cap.

He reached out. He put on his glasses with his other hand.

"Winks here," he said briskly, in his best Ass Manager's voice.

"So I hear," came the reply, in a voice that Bertie recognized at once without having to wait for the next words. "This is Quentin Kelly. Listen, Winks— we're in trouble. I want an extra five pounds from you or we're in the clag and right!"

Bertie knocked over one of his nearly full bottles of milk in his horror. Luckily it was six days old and set quite stiff.

"What?" he yelped.

"Five pounds," came the boy's voice. "And I'm not kidding, Winks. And, listen—don't get me wrong. It's not for me. I only wish it was."

"Well, who the——"

"It's for someone else. Someone who saw me plant some of that stuff. Someone who's blackmailing us. Says if we don't give him a fiver he'll go and spill everything to the Public Health."

It was no longer Bertie's day. The pin-ups might never have existed for Bertie now. And if one of those bluebottles had come near him just then he'd have snapped at it like a dog and swallowed it whole, still buzzing.

In fact, anyone watching might have thought he'd done it already, the way he was gulping. Then:

"Who?" he managed to say.

"Someone next door to where I planted that goldfish. Bloke. Old-age pensioner who says he could do with the money. And he means it, Winks—five pounds he wants, and if the cost of living goes up any faster he says it might have to be six."

"But——"

"Shut up! Listen! I think my old feller's just coming home. Heard the gate go. Can't talk about it any more just now. But listen, Winks. Quick. This is urgent. We've got to meet. Soon as possible. Talk it over. Agreed?"

"Yu-yu-yes, but——"

"Tonight, then. Nine o'clock. Somewhere quiet. And I've been thinking. Know that old bus shelter out at South Woods? . . . Good. Let's make it there then. Nine. O.K.?"

"Oh-oh-oh . . . kay!" gasped Bertie.

"Right. See you, Sheila!"

Bertie slumped back in his chair. It didn't strike him as being at all strange that the boy should address him as Sheila. He was cunning, that kid, and he'd say that to put his father off. Must have just walked in. Make him think he was chatting to a girl.

But—phew! . . . Bertie took off his glasses and sleeved away the sweat from his forehead. Was the whole story just another bit of cunning? Was the kid inventing this about the blackmailer to cover up a bit of blackmail of his own?

Bertie gave the phone a grim blue glare.

The bus shelter at South Woods, eh?

All right.

He'd be there.

But if that kid thought he was on to an easy five pounds, he'd got another think coming. Bertie was going to ask a few sharp questions, Bertie was. Nobody fooled Bertie Winks . . .

Meanwhile Quentin Kelly was helping himself to another slice of bread. He was a growing lad and this was his ninth. What was more, he was in a very happy mood and this gave him an extra-large appetite. He firmly intended to have another nine slices before he finished.

And why was *he* in such a happy mood?

Well, there was fried shrimp for tea for one thing. That was always a favorite with him. "Scampi for young scamps," his mother used to say—and since she always spoiled him she used to say it lovingly and offer him half of her own share. Which, being him, he always accepted.

And for another thing, there was the phone call he'd had earlier. Funny really. Right out of the blue. "This is the *Newsvendors' Journal*. We're happy to say your name's been submitted for our Newsboy of the Year contest—only one from every town—and we wonder if you'd mind answering a few questions . . ."

Mind!

Quentin Kelly smiled at the very thought. Answering questions was one of his strong points. So long as there was something to be gained by it. And especially if there was no need to be fussy about the *exact* truth.

So he had answered the questions and he'd enjoyed every minute of it, telling the man how careful he was with his deliveries. And if anyone is going to be Newsboy of the Year—he was thinking now—it's going to be me!

"*Quentin!*"

"Huh?" he asked, with a mouthful of bread, butter, and scampi.

"The *phone*, dear!" said his mother. "For you again. A gentleman who wouldn't give his name. I think it's the same one who——"

But Kelly was at the phone himself by now.

"Oh, it's *you*, Winks!" he said, a bit disappointed. "I——"

"Listen! Stop yappin' and listen! Somethin's gone

wrong . . . With the New Day job. It looks like . . .
we'll have to do it all over again."

The boy raised his eyebrows.

"Oh, it does, does it?" he said. "Well, unless you
settle up properly for *last* time, Winks, you've had
it!"

"Aw, don't be like that!" came the wheedling
voice of Winks. "You know I was gonner . . . settle
up. And for this . . . this next time . . . I'll give yer
. . . a fiver."

"Stop picking your nose, Winks, and say that
again, slowly!" said the boy. He felt much more
interested now, but still suspicious. If Bertie Winks

was as desperate as he sounded he might be willing to pay even more. But it would have to be in advance this time.

"But it'll have to be cash down," he said, when Bertie had repeated the figure, slowly. "And——"

"Aw right! aw right! We can settle the details later. There's a lot to tell yer . . . only, here, listen . . . I can't be telling yer *now*, over the phone. I don't know who might walk in . . . So listen . . . you know that old bus shelter out at South Woods? . . . Well . . ."

Chapter 19

THE BUST UP AT THE BUS STOP

The bus shelter at South Woods was a broken-down affair. The benches that had once lined its three sides had long since gone. Part of the roof had gone too. So had bits of the walls—where it looked as if some giant moth with steel teeth and a liking for asbestos had been biting holes. Even the broken glass from the vanished timetable frame had long since gone.

For the bus shelter was no longer in use. Not as a bus shelter, anyway. It had stopped being a bus shelter five years ago, when the Army had closed down the camp they used to have just behind the woods opposite. In fact, it wasn't used for anything much. Tramps preferred the old Army huts at the back of the woods. So did courting couples. So did the giant moth, judging from the state of some of those huts' walls. So the shelter was a very lonely place. An ideal place for the meeting that had been arranged. Deserted. Or deserted-seeming . . .

Deserted-*seeming*, I say, because, as everyone knows, in the first hours of darkness the fields and hedgerows come to life. Creatures begin to stir in the undergrowth. Movements can be heard among the weeds. Little gruntings. Little gaspings. Little scratchings. Little sighings. Little creakings. Little snufflings. Little groanings. Little burpings. Little growlings . . .

Quentin Kelly knew about all this. He was an intelligent lad. He'd read a thing or two. Before he'd got on to such books as *The World's Ten Great Tricksters* and *How to Live Lush Without Working*, he'd read quite a bit about nature. *The Little Furry Folk in Field and Hedgerow* had been one of his favorites as a child—especially the bits about weasels and snakes. So had *Out Walking with Uncle Tom and Wuffles the Dog*—even after he'd found out that Uncle Tom really didn't intend to murder the twins on one of their jolly nature romps. Quentin Kelly had a theory that Uncle Tom was nothing but a drunken old liar, really. He used to admire the way the man answered the twins' never-ending questions with a load of smooth old flannel.

So, as he stood there in the lonely shelter, peering down the road past the dark mass of trees, he wasn't at all worried by the tiny movements he could hear in the weeds behind the shelter.

A rustle? A field mouse.

A grunt? A badger.

A squeak? A shrew.

A hiss? A grass snake.

A clink? A——

Clink? At this point, Kelly did frown slightly, true. What creature could that be? he wondered. What creature was it that made a noise just like loose change clinking in a back pocket? Then he shrugged. Probably a rat treading on some rubbish in the ditch. Old nails. Bits of broken glass.

"And talking of rats," he said to himself, "where is he? Where's Winks got to? It's five past already."

As if in answer, there came the sound of an engine. Headlights flashed across the front of the shelter as the vehicle turned the bend in the road. They lit up Kelly, and Kelly's bike. And they sent the little creatures of the night scurrying for cover.

Then the vehicle drove up to the shelter and stopped. It was Bertie Winks in one of the dairy's trucks.

Now Bertie had been doing some thinking. And the more he'd thought about it the more strongly he'd felt that Kelly was trying it on. Trying to pull a fast one. Trying to scare him into paying out an extra fiver with this tale about a blackmailer. Of course, he couldn't be *sure*. He'd have to hear what the boy said. He'd have to make a few inquiries of his own. But in the meantime, Bertie had decided, nothing would be lost by taking a firm line. Showing the kid he wasn't easily scared. Letting him know right away what was what.

So he didn't greet the boy with a handshake on stepping out of the truck. He didn't smile and say how the nights were getting shorter. He didn't say anything about the shelter and what a shame it was that such an eyesore should be left in the town's green belt. He didn't go in for any fancy small talk at all.

He walked straight into the shelter and said: "Well, yer'd better get this straight right from the start. I'm not paying out no fiver to nobody—not if I can help it. An' that's flat!"

"Eh?"

Kelly was surprised. Kelly was shocked. Then, as Bertie started to say it all over again, Kelly became furious.

"You dirty little rat, Winks!" he cried. "You dirty little pop-eyed lopsided pink-nosed rat! You mean you've had me coming all this way for nothing? After you said straight out it 'ud be a fiver at *least*?"

Bertie nearly buckled the bridge of his nose, he gave it such a poke.

"Yer what? Don't you come *that* now! Don't you start putting words into me mouth, you lying little——"

"You mind your language, Winks," said the boy,

176

before Bertie had chance to get into gear. "Bluster won't get you anywhere. You said quite clearly, quite distinctly—a fiver. That's why I made you say it twice, remember? But I'm not going to argue with you. I'm telling you, Winks. It's a fiver or nothing."

Bertie was almost stamping with rage. He was pretty sure now that the boy was trying to trick him.

"You—yer don't get a penny! Y' hear? Not a penny. You're—you're nothin' but a——"

"All right! All right!"

The Kelly boy was at his sneering best. The angrier Bertie got, the cooler Kelly seemed to go.

"I might have known," he went on. "I might have known what it would be. You're a twister, Winks, a dirty little twister. You didn't pay me enough first time, did you? No, of course you didn't, don't butt in when I'm talking. You didn't pay me enough for the first lot. There was I, going round those doorsteps, round those bottles. Slipping a goldfish in here, a lump of glass there. And don't let me hear any more complaints about that goldfish, by the way. 'Overdoing it,' indeed! If I want to lend a touch of color to a dirty job that's my business." (He was a high school senior, remember, and when he got going he got going. Bertie was just stuttering by now.) "And anyway, the false teeth did the trick, didn't they? And whose idea was that, eh? . . . Anyway, Winks, don't you run away with the idea it was a picnic, it wasn't. It makes me sweat to think of it. I could have been caught as easily as that. And now I come to think of it, what if someone had been poisoned, eh? What if there'd been deadly germs on some of those things *you* gave me to slip in—like the glass and the cuff link? Eh? It's a wonder to me there wasn't, after they'd been in *your* pocket, you dirty little stinker!"

"Now you just listen to me! You was paid for that and you was paid handsome!"

"Handsome, he says! Handsome! Thirty bob! And he says handsome. Just listen to him!"

"*We have been!*"

"Just——"

Kelly stopped.

When he'd said "Just listen to him!" it had simply been a manner of speaking, of course. He had simply been addressing the gods, the Spirit of Justice— something like that. He hadn't been speaking to anyone in particular because, naturally, there wasn't anyone else there, besides Bertie. As far as *he* knew. . . .

He gaped at the tall dark figure that had just stepped around the corner into the shelter. So did Bertie gape.

"We *have* been listenin'!"

The figure dipped its head. Fire flashed from its hand. "Ow!" yelped Bertie, thinking he'd been shot. But it was only Louie, lighting his cigarette.

"Oh, it's *you!*" grunted Kelly.

"Yer, me!" said Louie, taking a deep drag of smoke. It had nearly killed him going without for the whole of twenty minutes. "We *have* been listenin'," he said again.

"We?" said Kelly, still pretty cool.

"Yes—me an' all!" said a smaller figure, coming around the corner and standing next to Louie. The light from the truck's side light gleamed in Smitty's rolling eyes.

"And me," added a third figure, coming and standing on the other side of Louie.

Kelly sighed. He even managed to grin. Tim Shaw, Smitty, Louie . . . What did it matter?

"Winks," he said. "I owe you an apology. We've been tricked."

"Guh! guh!"

Poor Bertie still hadn't got over the shock. Kelly gave him a leave-this-one-to-me slap on his shoulder.

"But it won't do them much good!" he went on.

"We heard everything," said Louie, with a low menacing tone that made him sound as if he wasn't sure which to go for first.

Kelly sniggered.

"And who's going to believe *you?*" he said.

"There's witnesses!" said Tim, unable to stand it any longer.

Kelly laughed outright. Even Bertie managed to stir up a gluey chuckle.

"What witnesses?" jeered Kelly. "*You* two?"

"Yer, fetch 'em out!" sniggered Bertie. "Less see 'em!"

Louie turned. He switched on a flashlight he'd been carrying. A powerful one that cut through the darkness like a spotlight.

"Tiger!" he called. "Feller wants to see yer."

Tiger Skinner stepped around from the back, into the spotlight.

"Detective-sar'nt Skinner, Chorburn Borough Police," said Louie.

Kelly and Bertie weren't laughing now. They backed away a little. Louie shot the beam behind them.

"Tub!" he called.

"Ah—at your service!" boomed Arnold G. Hooley, stepping around from the other side and looming over Kelly and Bertie like a well-dressed floodlit mountain.

"Oop!" gulped Bertie.

"Who——?" began Kelly.

"Arnold G. Hooley," snapped Louie. "Lawyer. Of Smith, Smith, Smith, Bagg and Hooley. Right, Tub?"

"Ah, one Smith too many, Lewis. But quite correct in principle."

"Sorry," grunted Louie. "Anyway. We was talking about witnesses. Them who's been listening. Every word . . . Nobby!"

This time, instead of a figure appearing, there came a voice. From one of the holes in the shelter wall.

"Glad ter see yer've got 'em . . . the rastals!"

Kelly jumped. It was the voice of Bertie Winks.

Then from another hole came another voice.

"Stop picking your nose, Winks, and stand up straight!"

Bertie jumped. It was the voice of Quentin Kelly.

"Show yourself, Nobby," said Louie, giving the flashlight an impatient wag. Then, as Norbert Rigg stepped into the beam, Louie announced him and Norbert bowed.

But this wasn't the end.

No fewer than four more witnesses stepped into the spotlight that night. All respectable men. All eminent men. All former members of Louie's Lot.

These were called out of the shadows and announced as follows:

"*Biddy!* . . . Major Bidolph Vickers, Third Battalion, the Grenadier Guards—second-best stacker I ever had.

"*Wogger!* . . . The Reverend Wallace Green, Vicar of St. Mary's, Ribchester—never slipped up once the whole time he was with me.

"*Chuck!* . . . Charles Peters. The Man They Couldn't Gag, columnist for the *Daily Pictorial*—had to keep telling him off for chatting on the route.

"*Faff!* . . . Mr. Ralph Cole, Chief Veterinarian at Battersbridge Zoo—wasn't a dog on the route didn't go off its food when he left."

And finally, with many a blush that showed up even in that light, there came Miss Jones with her notebook and pencil and the small shaded flashlight that Norbert Rigg had kindly held for her while she wrote.

"Everything you said," explained Louie sternly, giving his cigarette a flip in the direction of that notebook. "It's all took down in there."

Kelly and Bertie said nothing. They were still dazed, still wondering what had happened. It had been just like at a big fight. All these announcements. All these people stepping into the spotlight. It had been just like before a big fight, where famous people step into the ring to be introduced.

Except that these had stepped in *after* the fight.

Chapter 20

THE VICTORY ROUND

The rest is pretty well known by now.

Without going into all the old dry legal stuff, it can be said that Arnold Hooley handled the case beautifully. All the facts were checked. All the evidence was prepared—including all the things that Tiger Skinner had found out. Everything was typed neatly and put in the pink folder. Everything was sorted out and sworn to. The Public Health Department was informed and given a copy of all the evidence. And so were the local police.

The result was that when the case against New Day Dairies was called, it was automatically dismissed. The Public Health Department dropped the charge. Gilbert Dabbit himself had to get up and admit there'd been a grave mistake. Then someone else got up to say a much more serious matter had arisen. A case of conspiracy or something. With one or two more charges as trimmings.

Then everyone turned and looked at Bertie and Kelly, who looked pretty sick. And they were arrested the moment they stepped out of the courtroom—as they knew they'd be. The only reason they'd turned up at all was that their lawyers had told them to try and be as helpful as possible. It was their only hope.

And when *their* case came up, a few weeks later —well, they *were* helpful. They knew they hadn't a chance. They owned up. They apologized. They said it was a silly prank. They wore their best suits. Kelly even managed a few tears. But some people said they got off too lightly altogether.

Some said that Bertie ought to have been jailed. Even a fine as heavy as two hundred pounds wasn't tough enough for what he'd tried to do. But others said he'd been punished enough, getting fired from Rely-On-Us Dairies. Specially having to take the only job anyone would give him after that. Delivering coal. Where a bit of extra dirt wouldn't do much harm.

As for Kelly, opinions were mixed there too. Some said he wouldn't find it a picnic on probation with that new Scotsman they'd got. Others said they weren't so sure. Kelly was such a smooth talker it wouldn't surprise them if he didn't get the Probation

Officer into bad ways. Others again—and these were mainly the customers who'd suffered from the milk-nobbling—others again said it was time they brought back the birch.

But what of Louie in all this? After all, this kind of thing takes time to sort itself out. It might have taken ages for all his old customers to find out how wrong they'd been.

Fortunately, Louie took care of that right away. The morning after the bus shelter business he saw to it, with the help of Tim and Smitty, that the true story started getting around. And, just to give his comeback an extra boost, the men who'd answered the SOS put their heads together. Skinner, Hooley, Rigg, the major, the vicar, the veterinarian, and the *Daily Pic* writer—all put their heads together.

Imagine it. Seven heads, each with a wagging cigarette. All coming close together. It's a wonder they didn't burn one another's eyes out.

But they put their heads together and came up with a splendid idea. Really splendid. Then they went to Louie with it.

"Just for old times' sake," they said.

"And to give you and the Dairy some first-rate publicity to be going on with."

"I'll write it up in the *Pic*."

"Like a victory lap after a Cup Final. A victory *round*."

"Before we all go back."

"It'll be enormous fun!"

"A hit, man!"

And it was. The strangest delivery of milk the town had ever known.

A lawyer chatting up ex-customers.

A detective-sergeant stacking crates as fiercely as if they'd been stolen property.

A Guards officer helping him, doing it like rifle drill, calling out: "One-pause-two-pause-*crash!*"

A parson wondering if he could still jump over certain garden gates and regarding it as a challenge.

A veterinarian soothing up the savage dogs.

An actor, fooling about: being a Chinese milkman in one street, a vampire milkman in another, a love-sick milkman here, an idiot milkman there.

A newspaperman making notes of it all and wishing he'd got a photographer with him.

Tim and Smitty going purple with laughing.

And Louie blowing his top. Frothing so much at the mouth it nearly acted as a foam fire extinguisher and put out his cigarettes.

For, alas, his old helpers were out of practice. Obviously. By the end of the morning the full score was:

20 smashed empties;
15 tangled crates;
13 spilled fulls;
27 (twenty-seven) muddled orders; and
3 hours late.

Still, it *was* very good publicity. The very next day over half the old customers came back, and three hundred factory girls threatened to strike if the canteen order wasn't switched from Rely-On-Us to New Day. (They were hoping Norbert Rigg might come around again.) And, as Louie had to admit:

"You can't be good at everything, I suppose."

Even so, he gave Tim and Smitty a look when he said it—a look that told them they'd better not think *they* could get away with it.

At least not until they'd both become bishops or brain surgeons or something like that.

E. W. HILDICK is the author of over thirty books for children and teen-agers, three adult novels, and several critical books. Among the children's books are a number specially written for American readers, including *Manhattan Is Missing*, and he has also adapted several of his best British books for children in this country. These include *Louie's Lot*, which in 1968 won the Diploma of Honor of the Hans Christian Andersen Award Committee as the best children's book to come from Britain in the years 1965–66.

Before he began writing books, Mr. Hildick spent three years as a free-lance journalist and short-story writer. In 1957 he won the Tom-Gallon Award, one of Britain's premier short-story awards.

As a critic he has written for such journals as the *Times Literary Supplement*, the *Kenyon Review*, *Spectator*, and *The Listener*. In 1966–67 he was visiting critic and associate editor of the *Kenyon Review;* and in 1968–69 he was a regular novel reviewer for *The Listener*.

Recently he has turned his attention to the film and television fields, and is currently engaged in writing a series of television films based on his book *Birdy Jones*.